BLOOD REBEL

SIERRA ROWAN

Blood Rebel
Book Three of the Vampire Rebellion Series
by Sierra Rowan

© Copyright 2022 - Sierra Rowan
Published by Mountain Tree Press

Cover design by BZN Studio Designs
Proofreading by Kimberly Dawn and Happily Ever Author

ISBN: 978-1-955991-10-0

First published in 2022
Urbana, IL, USA

v.0.1

JOIN SIERRA ROWAN'S INSIDER'S CLUB

For the latest book updates, sales, giveaways, and more, join Sierra Rowan's Insiders Club at sierrarowan.com/subscribe!

AUTHOR'S NOTE

If you would like content guidance, please see the author's website at sierrarowan.com.

1

WREN

The sedan careened down the forest road, barely staying on the dirt track. On his motorcycle, Asher raced ahead of us, keeping an eye to the sky.

"Anyone following?" Liam called from the driver's seat, his damaged voice raspy.

I scanned the sky and forest, praying my vampire night vision meant I'd be able to see the shadowy forms of the rabids against the darkness. "I don't think so."

"What the hell just *happened*?" Mom demanded from the back seat, looking for all the world like she wished she had her service weapon with her—or any weapon, for that matter. Meanwhile, Dad kept glancing between the side window and the rear one, disbelief clear on his face.

I couldn't blame them. Not that long ago, they'd probably thought vampires were the stuff of fantasy. But now I was one, my sister currently sitting sandwiched between them was half-angel, and we'd all just survived the sadistic queen Amalie returning and somehow transforming the entire staff of the vampire hospital into rabids—those deranged creatures who cared nothing for life or civilization, only their next meal. Even the kindly doctor who'd helped me after I was bitten had just tried to kill us all.

How did I even begin to give them a logical explanation for that? I'd just been trying to help my parents. Something had put them under a spell, making them think I killed Harper and then later turning them into human statues. The clinic had been our only option to help them.

And then all hell broke loose.

"Liam?" I said, hoping he'd have a better idea how to respond. The Sentinel was over eight hundred years old, after all. Surely, if anyone had an answer, it'd be him.

But he just shook his head. "That shouldn't have been possible."

Silence followed his words for a few moments.

"What now?" Harper asked.

I didn't have an answer to that either. "Manor?"

Liam nodded.

"What manor?" my dad asked.

And there was *another* thing I didn't know how to explain, considering it involved demons and magic and a house that could be any size or configuration it wanted.

"It's this, um..." I chuckled, more desperation in the sound than anything, as I turned to face them from the front seat. "There's this couple. They're friendly"—Harper scoffed wryly, and I tried to ignore it—"and they'll help us. They have a house that's basically, um... well, it's like a fortress. No one can get in. No one else even knows it's there. They can help us stay safe."

"No, we need to get back into town," Mom said. "Head to the station. The police need to be warned—"

A protesting sound left Liam, and I shook my head. "Mom, the police can't—"

"Oh, my God," Harper gasped, staring at something past me.

Liam hit the brakes at the same moment his arm snapped out, his vampire strength and speed stopping me from flying forward. I turned, and my eyes went wide. At the junction where the track through the woods met the state road, a car was smashed into a tree, half blocking the road.

And it was on fire.

On the ground several yards from the car, a figure was sprawled. Two people crouched over them, and at the sound of our vehicles, they turned.

Blood soaked their chins. Fangs flashed in our headlights.

Asher was off his bike in a heartbeat, his knife appearing in his hand, summoned from whatever other reality it normally occupied. The blade glowed white against the night, and at the sight of him and the weapon, the rabids took off, shifting into shadow and leaping into the sky.

Leaving their meal.

Mom shoved the car door open immediately, ignoring my noise of protest. I scrambled out after her, a sword appearing in my grip the moment I was free of the car. I still had no clue what the blazing white blade of light even was. It'd just flared to life like an avenging angel in my grip when we were surrounded by rabids at the clinic.

One more question mark among *so* many.

Liam appeared at my side, his own knife in his fist. Trying to keep the sword from accidentally touching anyone, I hurried after my mom toward the wreck.

My stomach rolled at the sight of what the rabids had left of their victim. I didn't recognize the body, not that there was much still there to recognize. Their throat was gone. Parts of their face and chest too.

I looked up at the sky, searching for any sign of more rabids coming to attack. I'd thought I knew how vampires fed. I was one, after all. But this?

Surely, this wasn't normal.

"We need to call this in," Mom said, looking around like maybe the trees would sprout a phone. "We have to warn the police."

"And tell them what?" Harper replied. "Vampires are real, they can shapeshift into shadows, and that you just left a secret underground clinic where they all went crazy?"

Mom hesitated. "I don't know. But we have to warn people."

"You can't," Asher said, still watching the sky.

"I'm a police captain. I will not leave my town unprotected."

"Telling people isn't an option, for your daughter's sake as much as—"

"Excuse me?" Mom made an incredulous noise. "I don't know who the hell you all are, but what does protecting my daughter have to do with—"

"Mom!" I cut in.

She turned to me, furious.

"He's right," I said.

She stared at me.

"There's an organization out there called the GSS. Government Sanctioned Slayers. They'll kill us if they find out we're here. Me, Harper... maybe you and Dad too."

"And they've decided to help the ones who did this," Asher added with a gesture to the body.

I looked at him sharply. "What?"

He glanced at me, a grim expression on his face.

Oh, dear God, just when I thought it couldn't be worse... it got worse.

"Then we *need* to get the police involved to protect all of you," Mom insisted.

"We *can't*," Harper said.

"Why?"

I turned back to her. "Because we're talking about killers our own government is fine with, Mom. The GSS can do whatever they want. And they're brutal. Powerful. *Everywhere*. They kill... well, anything. Vampires, other stuff." My eyes twitched to my sister, the half-angel. Who knew what they'd think about her, considering she'd also been a ghoul at one point and then had some of my blood too.

God, when had our lives become this complicated?

I let out a breath, focusing. "The GSS made a deal with everyone nonhuman that as long as they all stay hidden, the slayers won't kill them. But anybody who's turned without authorization dies. Anyone who endangers humans dies. And if we go into town and start telling the police that *vampires* attacked us, and that I'm one of them... they'll probably make sure we die too."

My eyes flicked back to Asher as my stomach twisted with nausea. "And now apparently they're also working with Amalie."

Mom floundered, clearly searching for a way to argue.

"Please." I tried to keep my tone calm despite the way my heart pounded. "I know it's a lot, okay? But we need to keep moving, and we can't tell people what we saw or what really happened at the clinic."

"But those things are out here killing people," Dad protested. "Your mother has a point. We have to warn someone they're coming."

I glanced at Liam and Asher, not sure what to say. My parents weren't wrong, exactly. But the GSS would just kill *all* the rabids, and some of those creatures used to be our friends.

One of them might even be Ulysses.

My heart ached. The other Sentinel was out there, somewhere. Gideon too, hopefully. But Amalie had taken Ulysses' knife, and somehow because of that, she'd been able to turn him into a monster.

"Rabids are cowards," Asher said. "They strike at people who are alone."

I shifted my shoulders, thinking back on how they'd snatched me when I got separated from my friends in the forest weeks ago.

"Chances are," Asher continued. "This driver saw them flying and lost control of his vehicle out of fear, and they attacked him then. Whatever Amalie did to the staff at that clinic, it doesn't mean they'll do more than hide now."

"You can't know that," Mom countered.

"They know rabids, Mom," I said. "They fight them."

She looked away.

Harper made a hedging sound. "What if we just told the police you found out—I don't know—that there are addicts on some new drug? Warned the cops about that?"

Mom nodded immediately, latching on to the idea. "Yeah. They'd want to know how we knew, but... I could cover for that."

I hesitated, my eyes going to the night sky. God, it was risky standing out here arguing all night. Rabids could be descending on us this second. Or worse, Amalie could. Why the hell she hadn't already was anyone's guess, but we were still taking an awful risk.

But my family was also right. And maybe the GSS was on its way, regardless. Maybe the fact we'd warned the humans *without* giving the game away would matter to them.

"Okay," I agreed. "Let's just... Let's get out of here."

My family hurried to the car. Liam gave me a supportive look while Asher nodded to me and then climbed back on his bike.

A breath left me, and I got back in the sedan, trying not to grimace at the tense atmosphere. As Liam started the engine again, my eyes strayed to the corpse on the ground, guilt pressing on me. We'd send someone back for them. A cop, maybe, who could find the person's family and tell them... something.

Not the truth, though.

I scrubbed my hands on my thighs, trying not to feel like a terrible person for playing the GSS's game of keeping everything a secret. But would it help anyone to know vampires were responsible for this?

Or would it only make them scared?

In silence, we drove after Asher, winding down the state road. The victim's family would at least know their relative died, I supposed. If we hadn't stopped the rabids, the body might have been so destroyed that no one could've hoped to identify it, and then how much *more* pain would that have caused? So this was better than it could have been, even if we had to keep the truth a secret from—

We crested a rise, and my thoughts stuttered to a halt, my mouth falling open.

Oh, God, we'd been so wrong.

Fires burned in the city. Cars were wrecked on the road, smashed into each other like they'd been propelled one into the next. At the edge of the fancy neighborhood ahead, an SUV had somehow been put through the second floor of a house. Red and blue lights flashed past the intersection ahead, and even as I watched, another fire burst to life on the far end of town.

Chills spread through me. This couldn't be happening. I felt as if suddenly I was outside myself, like in the past few seconds, I'd just started watching a movie.

One that felt too damn real.

"Rabids wouldn't do this," Liam whispered as he pulled the car to a stop. "They *hide*. They don't..."

"Take us to the station," Mom ordered, her voice tight.

He started to shake his head.

"Now!" A frantic noise left her. "They'll have guns. The cells downstairs. It'll be safer than anywhere else."

He didn't move. "The manor—"

"Liam," I said, trembling. "We can't abandon people. Do it."

2

WREN

I'd seen so many movies, but none of them prepared me for this.

In silence, we drove into the city, watching every angle in case of attack. Streetlights were dead above us, casting the world in near darkness, and every house was dark. The power to the whole city seemed gone, and only the fires and my preternatural night vision let me pick out all the details.

Not that I wanted to see them.

Cars were thrown through windows, through roofs. On so many houses, the doors had been busted in, broken to pieces or torn from their hinges. The only mercy in all the destruction was that I couldn't see any bodies.

Maybe they just hadn't made it out of their homes.

Trembling gripped me, making my insides shake. "How many vampires were in the clinic?" I whispered.

Liam was quiet for a moment. "A hundred. Maybe more."

"Any rabids near town?"

He shook his head. "Just dormants."

A shaky breath left me. Dormants were the good ones. The regular folk who just wanted to live their lives in peace. But if whatever happened to the vampires at the hospital had—

A woman with long hair, tawny-beige skin, and utter terror in her eyes ran from the shadows between two houses, right at Asher, only to skid to a stop as his knife appeared in his fist.

"Please!" Her cry was muffled by the car window. "You have to help us!"

Liam came to a stop, a concerned expression on his face. "Dormant," he said without taking his eyes from the woman.

Warily, I climbed from the vehicle. "Stay here," I said to my family, praying my mom would actually listen.

"—my sister," I heard the woman say as I came closer, my attention as much on her as the sky and shadows around us. "She came home from the clinic, and she was a *rabid*! She said 'he' was calling us. That we had to be like her now."

"Slow down," Asher said. "She came to your house?"

The woman nodded, glancing at me and Liam before returning her focus to Asher. "Before she started destroying things with the others, she came to see us." The woman motioned behind her.

From the shadows, a smaller figure emerged. A boy with her skin tone and dark eyes, who couldn't have been more than fifteen. Even from here, I could see how he was shaking, but at the sight of the Sentinels, he tried to draw himself up like he was hiding his fear.

"She acted like she expected something," the woman continued. "Like we were supposed to *do* something when she got there or..." Her brow furrowed and she blinked, shaking her head hard. "We were supposed to have..."

Her hands went to her temples. "What... what is this?" She looked up at me as confusion filled her eyes. "He—" She stumbled back, horror taking over her expression as she gaped at me. "I can hear... oh, God..."

She cringed in on herself as the sense of wrongness that marked a rabid swelled around her. In the shadows, the boy fell to his knees, his hands gripping the sides of his head too.

"Shit." Asher motioned fast for us to retreat.

The woman straightened again, still watching me. The horror in her eyes faded.

Turning to hunger.

"Back to the car!" Asher ordered us, his knife raised.

Liam grabbed my arm, but I didn't need the encouragement. The woman lunged at me.

Asher caught her and flung her backward, but before she hit the ground she was already shifting into shadow and smoke. From between the houses, the boy stalked forward, his fangs bared.

I scrambled into the sedan, and Liam gunned the engine. In the side mirror, I saw Asher take off on his bike.

The woman hovered for a moment, and then both she and the boy surged into the air, getting lost against the smoky night sky.

"What the..." I looked at Liam. His mouth was set in a grim line.

"It's spreading here," Harper said.

I threw a glance back at her, my skin crawling. How far could this go? The city? The country?

The world?

"Th-the station is on First Street," Mom said to Liam. "You need to take Vine and turn onto—"

"I know."

Silence fell again. Adrenaline quivered through me as I scanned the houses and the sky. If anyone was inside the homes, they were hiding because I didn't see a single sign of movement.

Or they were dead.

My stomach twisted, and I swallowed hard. Hiding. We'd go with hiding. After all, I'd hide too if all hell started breaking loose in my town. So with any luck, everyone I knew—from students to professors to the baristas at my favorite coffee shop—was safe and fine and waiting out this nightmare in their—

A hoarse noise escaped Mom as we turned the corner onto First.

All my thoughts stuttered to a halt.

The station was engulfed in flames. Bodies lay before it, bloody and torn, with their badges and weapons glinting in the firelight. Several police cruisers had been stacked atop one another like children's toys. A few others were tossed into nearby buildings. The rabids seemed to love doing that.

Mom went for the door handle, and Harper reached out fast, stopping her.

An angry, frantic noise left my mother. "I have to—"

"They're dead," Harper said, her voice so tight that I could tell she was trying not to panic.

"Rabids might still be nearby," Liam added.

Gripping the door handle tightly, Mom didn't move.

Harper cleared her throat, working to hold her voice steady. "Ollie and Emma. We need to make sure they're okay."

Mom shook her head. "We need to find where the survivors of the police station are gathering."

I wasn't sure there *were* any survivors.

Liam made a cautioning sound. "We should regroup at the manor. Get you safe first."

I raked a hand through my hair. There were too many options, too many ways people we knew could be in danger. The manor meant safety, but driving away and leaving my friends was unconscionable. My best friend Brayden was probably okay, seeing as how he was out of town. Maybe okay, anyway. But Ollie and Emma...

"We need to know they're safe," I said to Liam. "The two of them helped us. We can't leave them. And they might have more info about what's going on," I added to my parents.

Dad frowned. "Honey, I don't think your college friends will know more than the cops would—"

"They're not human," Harper interrupted.

Dad blinked, falling silent.

"They're coyote shifters," she finished.

I glanced back to Liam, seeing the questions in his eyes. God, if we survived this, I was so going to learn sign language so he could communicate with me without hurting his throat through speech.

And maybe so everything I said wouldn't be overheard.

Shoving the thought aside, I gave him the address.

With a quick few signs to Asher up ahead, Liam started driving again. My heart was choking me by the time we pulled onto Ollie and Emma's street, and a whimper of relief left me to see their apartment building wasn't in flames.

Though that left so many other horrible options. I couldn't see any bodies here either. Short of the police station, I hadn't seen any at all. But that didn't mean—

I shoved the thought down hard. Hiding. People were *hiding.*

God, please let them be hiding.

"Hurry," Asher said the moment we left the sedan. His eyes on the sky, he clenched a fist as if resisting the urge to summon his knife.

My hands twitched, the same impulse moving through me. But the last thing we needed was a bunch of humans seeing a magical sword appear in my grip.

At least, not until I had no other choice.

"Hold it."

Asher's words brought me up short, but I didn't need the warning.

The door was ajar, and the security panel had been ripped from the wall. Beyond the glass panes, the electricity in the building seemed as dead as it was everywhere else. I couldn't see anything at all.

Trembling crept through me. God, what I wouldn't

give for a cell phone right now, if only to call and make sure my friends were still alive.

Asher nodded to Liam, who moved between us and the door while Asher continued closer. Reaching for the metal frame, he eased it open.

Darkness surged toward him, the sense of wrongness that marked a rabid coming ahead of it like a wave. In an instant, Asher's knife was in his grip, and he tore through the two shadows, sending them screaming into an oblivion of ash in his wake.

Silence fell. Nothing else moved.

"If the rabids have made it in here already," Asher said to me, and I could hear the unspoken statement that followed.

My head shook. Ollie and Emma wouldn't be dead. Our friends were shifters—not that I'd known that until about half a day ago. But they'd have picked up on what was happening better than the humans out there. They'd be okay.

"We have to check," Mom said.

Asher's lips thinned, but he nodded. Gripping the knife, he started into the pitch-black hall.

With a wary glance to Harper, I followed. My sister's angel nature was already starting to show through. Her hair and skin were glistening with that shimmer of gold they got when she was struggling to control her bizarre powers. But those bizarre powers had also saved our asses more than once, and without a word, she moved ahead of us, just in case she had to do so again.

Hopefully without hurting any of us in the process.

The emergency lights in the corridor had been torn

from the wall, but the ones in the stairwell were intact, and the white spotlight effect of them lit up the concrete steps in surreal relief. In silence, we hurried up to Ollie and Emma's floor, hanging back only briefly for Asher to go through the exit from the stairwell first. The emergency lights up here were intact as well, casting the hall in glaring light and deep shadow. At a quick gesture from Asher, he and Liam split up, each moving to guard the hall in either direction.

With a nervous glance to both men, I approached Ollie and Emma's door, praying nothing would jump out at us, and then knocked.

Silence answered me.

"Maybe they left?" Harper whispered.

I tried knocking again. She might be right, but it'd only been a few hours since we'd seen them, and they'd shown no sign of prepping to run.

Of course, the vampires in town hadn't been going mad then.

"Ollie?" I called, awkwardly trying to pitch my voice loud enough to be heard but not loud enough to carry. "Emma? It's us. Please, if you're in there, we're not like the others. I swear. We just—"

The door opened a crack. Ollie's face appeared in the gap, and I tensed. Her eyes were glowing like golden amber. Her teeth were sharp, more animal than human, and her lips pulled back from them in a snarl. A dusting of dark fur was like a shadow over what little I could see of her cheek, and the bone beneath was more pronounced than before. A low growl filtered out from her, making some primordial part of me want to fight or flee.

Oh, God, what if what Amalie did affected the shifters too?

"Please," I said, holding up my hands while the others backed away. "Ollie, if you can hear me in there, just... please don't listen to the voice. Fight it."

Her brow twitched down. "What?"

"The... the voice. Wait, what?"

Ollie's eyes darted over all of us, cautious. "You're not like them?"

My head gave a tiny shake.

"We don't know what's going on," Harper said.

A choked scoff left Ollie. She hesitated a moment more, watching us, and then eased the door back. "Get in, all of you. Quick."

Warily, I nodded for Harper to go ahead of me. Ollie studied us all as Mom and Dad followed my sister in, but when she looked past me, her eyes went wide. "What the—"

I threw a short glance behind me. "Um, this is Asher and Liam. They're—"

"Sentinels," Ollie filled in a bit hoarsely. "I know."

I wasn't sure what to say. She sounded like she was regretting opening the door.

"Thank you for allowing us into your home," Asher said carefully. "We mean you no harm."

"It's okay," I told her. "They're not like the others either."

Cautiously, she nodded and stepped back, giving them more room to pass. Emma stood in the living room, a single garlic bulb in one hand and a knife in the other, like a chef who'd abandoned the kitchen mid-recipe. Her eyes glowed gold like Ollie's but with a tinge of blue-green to the hue, and her face and arms showed traces of dark-brown fur. She gave a small gasp at the sight of Asher and Liam, and she held up the garlic bulb in a trembling hand while fear radiated from her.

I wondered what garlic did to us anyway.

"We're not here to hurt anyone," Asher said as Ollie shut the door and bolted it behind us.

Emma's eyes darted to her girlfriend while Ollie circled wide of us, sticking close to the wall, and then came to her side. "Why are you here, then?" Emma asked warily.

"We wanted to know if you were okay," Harper told them.

They hesitated. "Yeah," Ollie said. "No one has tried to come up—"

Shrieks broke out beyond the door, sounding like they were from somewhere lower in the building, closing in fast.

"Oh, crap," Emma whispered. She clutched the garlic bulb tighter.

A crash came from farther down the hall. Screams followed.

Liam was out the door before the sword could even materialize in my hand. Emma made a choked noise to see the glowing white blade in my fist, along with the knife in Asher's grip. Ollie just looked from me to the door and back again like she couldn't decide which to get farther away from.

Howls followed, receding fast. More crashing followed from deeper in the building.

My knuckles were white on the sword hilt.

Liam walked back into the apartment. Blood covered his hands and arms, prompting a strangled noise from Ollie, and for a moment, panic suffocated me at the thought he was hurt.

But I couldn't see a wound. His expression deadly, he signed something to Asher, who looked away, rage suffusing his face.

"What is it?" I asked. "What happened?"

It took a moment for Asher to respond. "They killed everyone."

A shaky breath left me. There was more to it than just what he said. I could hear it in his tone.

Asher looked over at Ollie and Emma. "Do you know any other vampires?"

They both shook their heads.

He nodded like it was some small relief.

"What's this mean?" Mom asked.

Both Sentinels were quiet again.

"Guys?" I urged. "What aren't you saying?"

"It means, if they're doing this elsewhere"—there wasn't much *if* in Asher's tone, more like utter certainty—"then anyone who ever asked a vampire to come into their home, either directly or by implication, could be a target. And anyone who leaves their house—say, because a car was put through the wall—will be too."

"What?" Harper breathed.

Asher's face was grim. "They're trying to turn the town."

3

GIDEON

With chains around my wrists, I hung from the stone wall and tried to plan for what came next.

I knew little of what had happened after my capture. Were the Sentinels still out there? Gods, I hoped they were, and I had to believe it was so. After all, I hadn't been destroyed by the blowback of our connection shattering through death. But I had scarcely any idea of where I was or how far from them I might be. There were no markings on my surroundings to give me a hint of my location. The floor below me looked like its carpet had been stripped away, only slabs of concrete with crusts of old glue remaining. The walls felt as if they might be artificial, the supposedly stone surface giving a hollow *thunk* that made it seem more like plaster than granite. Whatever this room had been, it was hardly a dungeon. More like a cheap farce.

But the chains around my wrists were certainly formidable.

My eye traced over the markings on the manacles. I recognized some of them. Old spells. Ancient ones. A few may have been for preventing someone from shifting form, while several more apparently suppressed my ability to feel the other Sentinels.

The latter was terrifying. The former was simply odd. That ancient vampire monster known as Urlfeige had stolen the power to shift into shadow from us when his people first kidnapped Wren weeks ago.

Why worry that I would regain it now?

The question was nothing more than a thought experiment, however. The reality was, whatever spells were carved in the steel, they also rendered me incapable of ripping them from the plaster wall. The gods knew I'd tried until my wrists had started to bleed. Likewise, I had stretched for my ability to feel for the other Sentinels, to tell where they were or if they were even still alive. The connection between us was deadened like someone had covered my eye and stopped up my ears.

It felt like being blind.

The door opened, and Amalie walked into the room like a debutante entering a ball. The satin of her blood-red skirts swished with her movements, and her nails and lips matched the color of the fabric. Her dark hair was swept back and pinned in such a way that left curls falling down her back in waves. In the time since I'd first seen her wearing this new body in a factory in Ohio, an indefinable quality had shifted in her face. None of her features had changed noticeably, the sharp lines remaining sheer and cold like she'd been carved by someone releasing their rage on stone. Yet her new body now looked more like the woman I remembered, rather than the woman who'd occupied it before Amalie took her over.

The effect was chilling.

"Ah, dear Gideon," she said as if just getting to me after a busy day.

I drew myself up, refusing to show any trace of fear.

But deep inside, I faltered when Ulysses walked through the open doorway behind her.

No chains bound him. He showed no sign of being a prisoner at all. No wounds marred his skin; his clothes were the same as I'd seen him in last. The pendant Asher had received from a witch and given to Ulysses—granting him the ability to fly and shift again after Urlfeige stripped us all of the power—that was gone. But in appearance, he seemed the same.

Yet the sight of him chilled me to the bone.

That was *not* Ulysses. I'd known him for over eight hundred years. He was as close to me as any brother, and as much as I would have died for him, he would have readily done the same for me.

But none of that man remained. Not the life in his eyes. Not the fiery personality, as quick to anger as to joke. The warrior who cared for the innocent and defended the weak was gone. Now he looked as cold and uncaring as stone. And yet the instinctive sense my own kind had upon looking at a rabid went mad when I saw him, my gut instantly shouting that he was one of them.

Transforming a vampire into a rabid was impossible,

and Ulysses had never been one of that ilk. Yet somehow, she'd managed it—or Urlfeige had.

I suppressed a shudder as Ulysses came to a stop, his dead eyes on Amalie as if he were a trained dog awaiting the command to attack.

"Oh, my pet, it's been far too long." Amalie sighed languidly.

She paced across the room while two other rabids came through the door. Both were easily approaching seven feet tall and dressed in black leather from head to toe. They wore motorcycle helmets to obscure their faces, the mirrored visors reflecting the room and revealing nothing of what was underneath. They possessed a chilling presence, as if violence was as close to them as my blade was to me—just beyond sight, ready at any moment to appear—and the wrongness pouring off them made the hairs on my arms stand on end. The force of it was stronger than in any rabid I'd ever seen.

"Do you like my new toys?" Amalie followed my gaze back to the rabids. "They're not *you* four, of course. But he did so want me to have more soldiers at my disposal, at least until you, Asher, and dear Liam are brought back to heel."

I pulled my gaze back to her, determined not to give her the satisfaction of thinking me scared to look at her.

She smiled. Her eyes ran over me, up and down, as if admiring the view. The rabids who'd chained me here had left me my pants and boots, but my shirt and eye patch were gone, baring all my old scars and the gnarled wound where my other eye had once been. As for the location of my weapons, I had no clue.

But I would be damned if I summoned my knife. Not when these accursed chains would only allow her to rip the blade away from me.

"Look at you," she said. "You think you've changed, don't you? You think you're... what? Some kind of hero to the people now?" She chuckled like it was a great joke. "The vampires don't need you, Gideon. They have *us*."

She glanced back at the open door with a smile, and I knew whom she meant. Urlfeige. The ancient vampire about whom almost nothing was known.

"I could let you talk to others, if you like?" she offered, her eyes blinking with feigned innocence. "The ones from that pathetic little clinic where they thought they were helping people. They could tell you how much better this is than the supposed *freedom* you protected for them."

"Spare me any more of your tricks," I ground out.

"*More* of my tricks?" Amalie turned back, an eyebrow raised, and her red lips pulled into a teasing smile. "My silly pet. Is this about the girl?"

She walked closer. "What? Did you think she was *me*? That I would pretend to be that pathetic scrap of a child?" She laughed as if I couldn't have been more foolish. "That little worm couldn't hold a candle to my power, much less possess it, and I'd never play at being anyone so weak. Surely you knew that?"

At my silence, she grinned. "Oh, my foolish toy. You saw a trick. I see an empty can, dented and weak and pointless without me. *Wren* was nothing more than a container, one who should have disintegrated when I abandoned her body, and one who will die *very* soon."

When she said Wren's name, it was as if she referred to

garbage that had attempted to cling to her shoe. But her disgust faded quickly. Reaching up, she stroked her fingertips along my cheek, and I fought not to show the revulsion that rolled through me at the feeling of her touch on my skin.

Like her face and body language, it was only too similar to the monster who'd enslaved me centuries ago.

"I can see you through her eyes, you know," Amalie murmured. "All her memories are mine, from the moment of her birth up until the day I discarded her body. Everywhere she went. Everything she thought. And you... oh, it stung her, what you said. Quite the cold bastard, weren't you? She thought you treated her like a pathetic little bug." Amalie chuckled, letting her hand fall as she turned away. "I'm so proud."

My insides quivered. It could be a trap. So many things had been during my years of captivity, from supposed allies to opportunities for escape. Over time, I'd come to distrust anything associated with Amalie because it was always just another one of her games.

But why insist Wren was nothing to her if the girl had been part of her plan? Why be *glad* I'd treated Wren so badly if she'd intended to bait me with her?

Could I have been *this* wrong?

Liam's words to me at the clinic echoed in my mind. *I'm not the only one she broke.*

But I had been so sure. After all, I'd wanted Wren. Craved her in a way that defied logic, which was enough to cause concern all on its own. And true, I'd never felt *attraction* for Amalie. Quite the opposite. The queen had used any number of spells to get us to submit to her—for the gods knew we'd never been willing. Yet Wren had only to *look* at me to rouse my blood and fill my mind with erotic fantasies.

But Amalie had bound us to herself centuries before, and the queen's soul had been inside Wren's body. The threat had been too dangerous to ignore.

It made sense at the time. I'd been a bastard, yes. But I'd believed there was good reason.

And now Amalie was *proud*...

She turned back to me, and my spiraling thoughts skidded to a halt as she withdrew a weapon from the folds of her skirt. I recognized it immediately, seeing as it was a twin of my own blade. Ulysses' knife. The metal was dull now, without a trace of the glow it sometimes held. It looked cheap, like false weaponry purchased from a costume store. Still metal, yes. Still potentially sharp. But without any of its luster. A thread of thin black wire coiled around the hilt, and even if I couldn't identify the material, the magic coming from the binding was easily discernible.

Ulysses showed no reaction to her holding the blade, his dead eyes not even bothering to turn in its direction.

"Why hang on to this silly illusion of freedom?" Amalie asked, turning back to me. "Why cling to pain and suffering, when you can—"

The door opened, and a rabid rushed into the room, his head tucked low. "Apologies, Mistress. Apologies, apologies."

Irritation flashed over Amalie's face, an expression I knew could portend death even for the mildest annoyance. "What is it?"

The man stopped about a dozen feet away, not answering.

Amalie whirled around, the knife still in her fist. "*What*? I'm having a conversation."

He nodded, his eyes flashing between me, Amalie, and the floor.

With an impatient huff, Amalie stalked over to him. "Your skin would make a halfway decent covering for the wall. Speak or I'll begin carving."

His eyes widened. In a frantic whisper, he relayed his message, his voice low enough that I couldn't catch it all.

"—not working... Master says... the girl."

My brow twitched down. Wren? Did they have her? Nothing about the atmosphere of the room seemed to reflect that.

If anything, it was only becoming more volatile.

"—Master says... need to find... now."

For a moment, Amalie didn't move. Her shoulders rose and fell in controlled breaths. Her grip adjusted on the knife, the motion automatic and repetitive.

My skin crawled. I knew this. The moments before her rage would explode.

"That—" A breathless chuckle left her. "No. She is *not* the one he needs to..." The chuckle came again. I didn't dare move lest she drive the knife through my chest to assuage her anger.

The rabid had no such prudence. "What would you have us—"

His head hit the floor. The rest of his body took a moment before it followed.

Amalie stalked toward the leather-clad rabids by the

door as the man disintegrated into dust behind her. "Ulysses!" she snapped without turning around.

Like a dog, he followed her, no trace of reaction on his face.

Her savage whispers were too soft to hear. Ulysses shook his head. She snapped something else. The enormous rabids nodded and then left the room.

Amalie remained, knife in hand, shoulders rising and falling.

I braced myself.

"So, tell me..." She turned, regarding me with a tight smile that sent shivers all the way to my bones. "Where is the girl?"

At my silence, she chuckled again, the sound barely in control. Apprehension boiled to a fever pitch inside me.

"My darling Gideon." She walked toward me, her skirts swishing. With the same brutal smile, she wove the knife back and forth through the air, though the dull metal barely reflected the light. "Always the stoic one. Not like Asher. He was a soldier. Disciplined. Trained not to cry out, at least not easily. You?" She chuckled softly. "You just thought your mind could hold you separate from the pain."

She came to a stop in front of me, her eyes on the knife. "Where would my disobedient pets take the girl?"

At my silence, she glanced up from the weapon to regard me.

"I *will* find her, Gideon. The moment she goes anywhere familiar, she'll be mine. I have her memories, after all. There's nowhere she could think to go that I won't find. So your silence doesn't spare her. All you're doing is making sure those around her suffer as well."

My jaw tightened.

"Do you really want to gamble Asher's and Liam's lives?" The pinprick of the blade's tip rested against my abdomen. "Do you want to gamble your own life if they die?"

Lightly, she drew the blade up, leaving a bleeding line scarcely deeper than a paper cut.

"You know I love hurting you," she whispered. "But I also know how it pains you to watch me hurt the others. I'll never forget the night I took Liam's voice. The horror in each of your eyes. Or"—she lifted the blade, placing it on my cheekbone—"in your case, *eye.*"

I held my face still, but I couldn't stop the way my heart began to pound. That night had been hell. Hearing one of our number screaming in her chambers had been familiar after so many years of torture, but when his cries cut off... when her servants brought him back to us, dumping him on the stone floor with his throat so badly savaged no amount of blood or healing could ever restore it fully...

Once upon a time, he'd had the most beautiful singing voice any of us had ever heard.

I kept myself from glancing down toward the blade resting beneath my one remaining eye. Everything changed that night, when I realized what she was truly willing to do to us. *How* horrifically she was willing to maim even her prized Sentinels, all for fun.

If she were to make me blind...

Her smile returned. "Where's the girl?"

Gritting my teeth, I held my tongue, no matter how terror beat around inside me like a trapped animal. But I wouldn't throw the others to the proverbial wolves. I had more honor than that.

And if Wren truly was an innocent…

The knife bit into my cheek. "Where is she, Gideon?"

"Go to hell."

Her expression turned chiding. I didn't move a muscle, the blade resting mere centimeters beneath my eye.

Amalie chuckled, withdrawing the weapon as blood dripped down my cheek. "I know what you're afraid of, but I think I should save that treat for later, don't you? Instead, how about we start with you summoning that fascinating knife of yours? Show me that lovely blade. Is it like the one my dear Ulysses had?"

My eye darted to my fellow Sentinel—or whatever he was now. He hadn't moved, and the utter lack of expression on his face was unchanged. He may as well have been watching a blank wall for all the interest he showed.

There was nothing of my friend and ally in that gaze.

But if he hadn't told her where the others would try to take Wren…

Hope flared in me. It wasn't much, not in the face of whatever magic had been wrought upon him, but if somehow Amalie or Urlfeige couldn't force him to reveal things his *true* self would never have shared, perhaps something could still save him.

But I needed more information.

"Oh, he won't help you," Amalie said. "Not now that he's been returned to his proper nature."

"What have you done to him?"

"My pet? Nothing." At my expression, she laughed. "Oh, Gideon. For all your reading, you're really quite foolish. All this…" She gestured as if to encompass everything I was. "This care? This compassion? This *humanity* you all play at?" She said the word like it was a joke. "It's an aberration. But we fixed it. We set it back to the way it was. The way it always should have been. Before her."

My brow twitched down. "Before whom?"

Amalie grinned. "You'll see. You'll be like dear Ulysses soon. The moment you summon that knife, this foolishness of yours will end, and you'll understand."

My eye flicked to Ulysses. Was that how they'd done it? Were our knives protection somehow, at least as long as they were in our possession?

She chuckled. "Always so resistant—at least at first, yes? But you *will* summon it. I guarantee you will." She leaned in close, her lips only a few inches from my ear. The blade came to rest just above my heart. "The power he's given me… what I can do to you… Oh, Gideon."

The knife bit into my flesh, and she made a pleased noise as blood trickled down my chest. Leaning back, she smiled.

Striations of dark shadow swept over the whites of her eyes like black ghosts.

I tensed, fighting to hide my shock. What in the hell was that?

An amused sound left her. "I promise, my pet. None of you are stronger than me."

4

WREN

The hours until sunrise were the longest of my life.

I jumped out of my seat the moment the door to the apartment opened. Liam came back in, his expression grim.

He signed something that took a few seconds to finish. Asher shook his head.

"How many?" I asked.

"Two more apartments, possibly. Six houses too. But they're taking the bodies, so he can't be sure whether they..." Asher grimaced.

"Whether they killed them or turned them," Harper finished hoarsely. "Right?"

He nodded.

A desperate noise left my mother. It'd been all we could do to keep her here as Liam patrolled and the hours passed. Only telling her Harper or I would go out there too if she tried to leave seemed to keep her from barreling out the door to help people.

Not that there was anything to do. The rabids were breaking into homes and tearing into people. How could she stop that?

The lights clicked on and the television flared to life, making me jump.

"Power's back," Dad said. "That's a good sign, yeah?"

No one answered. I didn't want to think about what had probably happened to the workers who'd tried to get it going before sunrise.

"Check the news," Mom said to Dad. "If this happened anywhere else…"

He retrieved the remote from the couch nearby. "Want to see if the phones are back too?"

"Yeah." She glanced at me. "Can you ask your friends if we could try their cells again?"

I nodded. Mom and Dad had been trying to call anyone they knew, just to see if they were okay, and Harper had done the same, but so far, we had no idea who out there was still alive. The cell towers were either overwhelmed or torn down. No calls were getting through.

Nausea twisted through my insides while I headed for the kitchen. My best friend Brayden was in St. Louis for a music conference. He'd be okay. Assuming this hadn't continued to spread, anyway. As for everyone else in our lives… How likely was it they knew any vampires?

I didn't want the answer to that question.

"—get out of here and—" Ollie cut off. "Oh, hey, Wren."

I stopped at the entrance to the kitchen, trying to refocus past my spiraling worries to concentrate on why I'd come to see my friends. A mug of coffee was in Ollie's hand; Emma was pouring her own, and I had distinct impression I'd interrupted something.

"Um, sorry." I hesitated. "Everything all right?"

Emma cast an uncomfortable look to Ollie. "My parents got through on my cell a minute ago. They're okay. Ollie's too. No sign of vampires acting like this where they all are, but..." She winced.

"They want us to come join them," Ollie filled in. "A couple of shifter families aren't willing to wait and see if this spreads. They're heading for, um..." She bit her lip, glancing toward the living room like she didn't want to be overheard.

I didn't know what to say. They were both still wary as hell of the Sentinels, watching them like they expected Asher or Liam to turn rabid and attack them at any moment.

"Where?" I asked softly, stepping closer and then freezing when they both tensed.

It wasn't just the Sentinels they were worried about, then.

I buried a grimace and didn't come any closer.

Emma glanced at Ollie, her brow twitching up like she was making a silent point.

Ollie frowned, but she turned back to me and said, "Gateway City."

My brow furrowed. "Huh?"

She threw another look toward the living room. "One

of the underground cities. Shifters and all kinds of people live there in caves and stuff. Humans can't get in. And, um, after the wards they put up in a rush last night, now vampires can't either—at least, no more than the ones who were there already."

I stared at them, still reeling from the idea there were cities full of supernatural creatures underground.

"Lots of the shifters are heading there," Emma said apologetically. "But, you know..."

"No more vampires allowed," I filled in.

She winced and nodded.

"We tried to tell them you all weren't like the others," Ollie said. "But nobody's taking the word of a couple college students, you know? Not given what happened here and at the clinic last night. They've even got the vampires in Gateway on lockdown too, just in case."

My skin crawled. "Did they say if this was happening anywhere else?"

"So far, no." Emma looked uncomfortable. "At least, not yet."

"I'm sorry," Ollie started. "I—"

"It's okay." I drew a breath, trying to put a smile on my face. "Really. Now that the sun's up, it'll be a lot safer anyway. We can just head back to where Asher and Liam live. We'll be fine."

Ollie's brow twitched down. "But the sun...?"

Right.

"Asher and Liam aren't affected by it, and they can extend that to me."

Emma made a worried sound. "That's *real*? They actually can go out in the sun and not... you know?"

I nodded.

"I thought that was just a story people told about the Sentinels," Ollie said, staring at me as she set down her mug.

"It's *just* the Sentinels who can go out in sunlight, though, right?" Emma pressed. "And... and you, for some reason?" She hesitated. "Are they why you're a vampire? Did they bite you?"

"No." I shook my head quickly. "It... it's complicated."

I prayed they wouldn't ask for more information, considering my protection from the sun involved a connection to the Sentinels that still didn't make any sense to me. Amalie was gone from my mind, but my tie to the Sentinels remained somehow. If anything, it felt stronger, but in a lopsided way. Like somehow Asher and I shared more of *whatever* was between us than I had with Liam.

And given that, of the two of them, Asher was the one I'd fed from and the one I'd had sex with...

"Listen," I said, hoping I wasn't blushing no matter how my cheeks were starting to burn. "I just came in here to ask if we could borrow your cell—"

"*Shit.*" Asher's voice carried from the living room.

I emerged from the kitchen to find him turning away from the window, yanking the curtains closed behind him with his knife already in his fist.

Fear bubbled through me. Oh, God, what now?

"Check the hall," he said to Liam.

The other Sentinel nodded and strode past me to disappear out the door.

"You have any more garlic in the house?" Asher continued to Ollie and Emma beyond me.

Nausea gripped me. God, no. It was *daylight*. Surely...

Ollie's head shook. "Just that one we found in the pantry. We're not even sure how old it is."

"I thought you all said the..." Dad struggled with the word. "The vampires couldn't come out during the day?"

I hurried across the room, and Asher moved to block me as I went for the curtains. "If they see you—" he started.

"It's just as bad as if they've seen you."

He scowled but stepped back, peering past the far edge of the curtain. I took the other side, careful not to make much of the fabric move as I peeked around it.

Six enormous figures stood beside motorcycles in front of the apartment building. Dressed like some kind of post-apocalyptic nightmare, each of them was huge, and every inch of their skin was covered in black leather. Even their eyes were protected by motorcycle helmets with the visors pulled down. The wrongness of rabids radiated from them, making my stomach churn, and with their masks, their facelessness made them even more terrifying.

"What do we do?" I asked Asher.

"They might not know we're—" He cut off as one of the enormous vampires pointed straight at our window. "Oh, hell."

I stared, fear freezing me. How could they see us? We should be basically invisible up here. Unless...

Dread sank over me, the answer coming to me with horrific clarity. Amalie had been in my head. I'd seen her memories.

How many of mine had she seen?

The rabids ran for the apartment building's door. I stepped back quickly, looking around the room. My family stared at me, and my friends did too. There wasn't another way out of here.

And the rabids were coming.

5

ULYSSES

I was a prisoner in my own body, and Hell was fighting to claim me.

A whirlwind of noise and smoke surrounded me. Reality was a light ahead of me, like a sun fighting to break through the clouds, but the storm kept trying to drag me away from it, back into the darkness. My mind felt like a terrain scoured down to rock by the winds blasting me, and I clung to the rough surface by my fingernails, struggling not to be swept away.

I couldn't let it take me. I knew that down to my bones.

Even if I wasn't actually able to feel my body anymore. The whirlwind had already taken that over, stealing sensation from me when I was knocked backward from the light that was reality into this dark place in my mind. And without a grip on the light, I couldn't control what my body did anymore.

Fear pulsed through me about that. The storm had taken command of my body, and the gods only knew what that meant. Past the whipping winds, I could only catch flashes of the real world. A room with no furniture. A hallway. Maybe Gideon, but I wasn't sure. Sound was hard to make out as well.

At least, sound from the reality outside my mind. Voices swirled endlessly through the storm, vivid and vicious, despite the fact that I couldn't *actually* be hearing them.

Because they were dead.

"...failed us..."

My father.

"... your fault..."

My sister.

Snarling, I fought to claw my way through the storm. If I could only make it back to the light, I knew I could reclaim command of my body. Wren was out there somewhere. Asher, Liam, and Gideon too, and dammit, I needed to help them. There'd been rabids flooding the halls. An attack coming at us.

Where had there been an attack?

I cursed, trying to focus, but the storm winds were made of knives, cutting into me, carving things away. And the harder I tried to hang on, the deeper they slashed, until it felt as if my mind was bleeding.

"...why didn't you save them?"

Grief cost me an inch of my grip, and the hurricane howled at its momentary victory. That was little Calliope, my niece. The only survivor of the night Amalie murdered everyone else I loved, just to get me to submit to being bound to her over a thousand years ago.

Dark laughter rolled through the whirlwind, and

instinctively, I gripped harder on the rough terrain of my mind. *That* wasn't a voice from my distant past. It was Urlfeige, the creature we'd heard that night the rabids kidnapped Wren. The one who'd stripped our powers to fly and shift into shadow from us, sending us crashing down into the forest below as if we were rocks dropped from the sky.

It was a nightmare.

"Surrender."

The voice reverberated through the entire storm, stronger than any of the words of the dead. My grip shuddered, the terrain of my mind quaking from the sound.

"You won't win this."

I dug my hold in deeper. "Fuck you."

The laughter struck like a whip, and pain exploded through me. My grip faltered, and the wind flung me backward instantly. Frantically, I clawed at the ground, fighting to regain my hold.

Stone thudded into my back. Twisting, I caught sight of a rough wall behind me like a cliff face of dark stone, all of it threaded through with faint strands of light.

And nearby, a cave.

I dragged myself toward the refuge as the wind howled, scathing and filled with the voices of the dead. But the ferocity faded as I hauled myself into the shelter of the opening.

For a moment, I could only shudder in the shadows, one hand braced on the wall. Images flashed at the corners of my eyes. Nights spent relaxing at the manor, all of us watching movies in the theater room. Asher cuing up a marathon of classics. Liam grinning at a joke. Gideon critiquing the historical accuracy of the plot. Good times, all of them playing back as my hands brushed over the wall. This was my life. My history embedded in the stone of my mind. I couldn't let this bastard take it from me.

The cave around me shuddered. Rocks fell from the walls, vanishing into smoke before they hit the ground.

And the wind shifted, reaching into the cave, chasing me even here.

"Surrender."

The voices of the dead followed the command, swirling like hunting dogs ready to be unleashed. The ground shook as the wind picked up, whipping around me like ghostly hands, tugging me back toward the cave opening.

Hell no.

Without another option, I spun and took off into the shadows of the cave. The tunnels twisted, incomprehensible. Everywhere I went, more memories flashed past me —old friends lost to the centuries, the time we rescued Friday and Barnaby, the fire Eden still blamed us for, and rightly so—all of them turning to smoke as rocks fell from the walls.

Desperation pounded through me. I couldn't lose this place. It was everything I'd ever been. I needed somewhere to hide and regroup. To figure out how to fight this thing.

And then, somehow, I had to find my way back to the light.

6

———————

WREN

"What do we do?" Dad asked.

"Grab anything you need to take with you," Asher said to Ollie and Emma. "Do it fast."

Emma's mouth moved as she blinked. "Okay, um—"

Ollie raced for the bedroom.

"We'd been packing," Emma explained weakly, looking around like she was wishing she had more than the single bulb of garlic in the house.

Ollie emerged a moment later with two stuffed backpacks, one purple and one teal. Wordlessly, Emma took the purple one.

"Come on," Asher said, heading for the door. "Stay behind me."

His eyes landed on me as if to emphasize his point. I gritted my teeth, and my hand flexed, but I resisted the urge to summon the sword. In the tight hallway with my family and friends all around me...

Shivers ran through me. I couldn't risk hurting them, even if only by accident. But that didn't mean I couldn't be ready to call for the thing if needed.

I gave Harper a quick glance, and without a word, we both moved to keep our parents behind us. Ollie and Emma brought up the rear, backpacks on their shoulders. At the door, Asher leaned his head out briefly, glancing back and forth, and then nodding at something. Maybe Liam signing to him from his position in the hallway. But a moment later, Asher stepped out into the hall too and motioned for us to follow.

No sound came from either end of the corridor as I left the apartment. The hallway lights were on, and through a window at the end, daylight thinned the remaining shadows. But too many dark patches still clung to the hall for my comfort. I couldn't feel the wrongness of rabids coming from them, but that didn't stop me from worrying.

At the door to the stairwell, Liam made short gestures to Asher, who gave another nod. Seamlessly, they moved together, Asher shifting his stance, ready to strike, while Liam took the handle.

Shadows lunged into the hall the moment he pulled open the door.

I was no expert, but immediately I could tell these weren't regular rabids. Twin shadows moved like lightning, whipping past Liam and Asher, and malevolence just *radiated* from the pair of them. They seemed to be everywhere the Sentinels' weapons were not, darting around the men like they were perfectly in sync and knew exactly how to avoid their blades.

Asher snarled a curse, spinning around in an instant. "Get down!" he shouted at us as the shadow shredded the air, heading right for us.

My sword surged to life in my hand, but still I ducked with the others. Liam lunged at the rabids, leaping past us with his blade drawn. The shadows twisted toward us, and I'd swear they were reaching right for me. But Liam twisted too, somehow managing to shift his trajectory even if he never shifted form, and his knife slashed through the air, catching the edge of one rabid. The creature howled, stalling its motion for less than a heartbeat.

But it was enough. Asher threw his knife, the weapon ripping through the rabid and slamming into the wall behind us. As the first rabid died, the second jerked up toward the ceiling to hover there. Even without a face, I'd swear it was snarling at the Sentinels.

Asher's lip twitched, his eyes never leaving the creature, as his hand made a short, twisting gesture, as if yanking something back. The blade in the wall vanished. Nearby, Liam had his weapon still drawn, watching the rabid but staying close to us.

The creature stayed put for a moment, pure hate emanating from it, and then tentacles of shadow began spreading from its core down toward me, twisting to evade me when I whipped the sword toward it. A panicked noise left Harper, and her blond hair started to glow.

Asher's eyes never left the other vampire. Flicking his wrist again, his weapon reappeared, sailing back through the air toward him.

Right through the rabid.

The shadow screamed as the blade slashed through it,

the metal glowing bright as if it was lit from within. Asher snagged the weapon from the air while, like smoke without a fire, the creature disappeared.

With a quick nod to Asher, Liam headed for the stairwell.

Asher glanced back at me, and then his eyes flicked down to my sword. I clutched it tightly, not sure what to do. I'd fought rabids in Cincinnati, my body reacting even though my brain never caught up, but I couldn't exactly control that. And he didn't know about it anyway.

But all he said was, "Stay behind me." Gripping his knife, he motioned for us to follow.

"My car is behind the building," Ollie said, her voice unsteady. "Ground floor, just left of the—"

A shriek came from beyond the door, and a dark shadow slammed into Liam, tearing him away from the stairs and into the chasm at the center of the stairwell.

"Liam!" I cried, racing for the opening.

Asher caught me with an arm around my middle, and my sword vanished instantly rather than hit him. From beyond the door, I could hear enraged and pained shrieks echoing, but I couldn't tell if any of the cries came from Liam.

Another shadow appeared at the doorway, shifting form into a towering figure covered head-to-toe in black leather and a biker helmet with the black visor still pulled down. Asher shoved me behind him quickly and raised his weapon.

I'd swear the rabid was grinning at us, even if I couldn't see it past his visor. "Sentinel," he hissed. "Last one standing. My ally has just killed your companion, so surrender, and she'll let you—"

Soft and fast, I barely heard the footsteps before suddenly, Liam raced up the stairs behind the vampire. The rabid started to turn, but Liam was already there. His hand gripped the creature's helmet, yanking it backward faster than the rabid could move to fight him, while his other hand held his blade.

I flinched but couldn't turn away quickly enough to avoid seeing the glowing knife tear into the rabid's neck so deeply it took his head from his shoulders.

The creature collapsed, leaving Liam standing in the doorway, ash of the dead rabid fluttering down around him.

Relief that he was alive hit me like a two-by-four, but worry was right on its heels. Bloody cuts showed on his cheeks and neck like he'd gone a few rounds in a knife fight. A feral light shone in his ice-blue eyes, wild and dangerous. But he paid his wounds no attention as he signed something to Asher that even I could understand.

Four down, two to go.

Assuming more hadn't arrived.

Asher gave a dark look toward the other end of the hallway. Now that the electricity was back, I knew the elevator was an option, but anxiety still spun up like bees inside me at the thought. Sure, it'd get us to the first floor faster. It also trapped us all in a box at the mercy of electricity and any rabids who might try to get inside.

Or cut the cables.

Asher apparently came to the same conclusion. "Stay

close," he said to us. His free hand took mine, keeping me with him as he headed through the door.

The air inside the stairwell was clammy, and even though my family and I tried to stay quiet, the sound of all our steps on the concrete stairway still bounced off the cinderblock walls. Stale smells of old take-out food and body odor hung around us, along with something harsh and charred that didn't require much of a leap to guess its origin.

Dead vampire.

Shuddering, I hurried toward the ground level, my eyes flicking around the stairwell. Dark smears of ashes clung to the walls erratically, ending in a pile of blackened dust at the base of the steps. Evidence, I guessed, of what happened to the rabid stupid enough to attack Liam.

"Glad they're on our side," Dad murmured when we reached the ground floor and passed a disintegrating pile of ash.

Asher's lip twitched, but his humor vanished fast as Liam stalked toward the door.

No rabids waited in the hallway beyond the stairwell. To my left, sunlight glowed past the turn, suggesting the way out lay in that direction. To my right, the corridor was empty. Just a line of doors on either—

A clang came from beyond the turn to the exit, like the metal-framed door hitting the wall, and a shriek followed. A backpack hit the floor at the corner, spilling books everywhere. A rabid in full leather and a helmet hauled a struggling young woman into view, his hand gripping her arm so hard she looked like she was crying out as much in pain as fear. Keeping her ahead of him, he started down the hall toward us, and once he was beyond the direct light from the door, he ripped the helmet from his head. His scalp was shaved hairless, and his dark eyes were anything but sane. His fangs bared even as his pale skin began to smoke in the ambient light, and he bent his head to keep the woman's throat near his teeth.

"Stand down, Sentinel." He grinned around his fangs. "Your kind care so much for the cattle. Careful, or your pretty girl will watch you lose one." His eyes went to me. He flicked his tongue along the woman's neck, and she whimpered.

A chuckle came from behind us. I threw a frantic look back to see another rabid blocking the other end of the hall.

"No way you get to me before I kill her," the first rabid said, his fangs only inches from the woman's skin. "And if your little friend with the glowing hair tries anything, I'll take out this one's throat before she dusts me."

Tears rolled down the woman's cheeks.

"What do you want?" Asher growled.

The rabid's eyes swept me and Liam before returning to Asher. "Her." He nodded at me. "His missing piece."

My brow twitched down. "What?"

His lips curled back from his fangs. "Pollen, pollen carries the bumblebee. And wherever she goes, she sets us free."

Chills coursed through me. I had no idea what the hell he was talking about, but at that knowing look in his eyes, all I wanted to do was run like hell.

The rabid turned his grin on Asher. "We'll take you

two as well, if you're not dust. Finish out the set her highness has started."

My stomach clenched. He had to mean Gideon and Ulysses.

Asher shook his head. "Not happening."

One eyebrow rising, the rabid leaned closer to his captive. "You sure about that? Your friends have already joined us. They're feasting as we speak. You think you can hold out against our master where they didn't?"

Horror turned my blood to ice. God, no…

"Release her *now*," Asher ordered.

"Not a chance." The rabid tightened his grip on the girl. "I can smell this thing's blood. Fear makes it taste even better. Surrender or add this one to all the others on your conscience. All the ones whose blood are feeding your friends right now."

Asher's expression was as cold as I'd ever seen it.

The rabid grinned. "Come on, Sentinel. Offer won't last long. I'm hungry."

Behind us, the other rabid shifted from one foot to the other, as if halfway to dancing with his anticipation of tearing us apart.

Another clang came from the exit door beyond the turn, as if the metal frame had been yanked open again, and the sound of heavy footsteps followed. A motley assortment of men and women raced around the turn. "Hey!" one of the guys shouted.

The rabid holding the young woman glanced back, his fangs bared.

Liquid from a jar splashed into the rabid's face. Crying out, he recoiled.

The group charged at him. A brunette woman grabbed his captive, tugging her back as two of the larger men shoved the rabid at the wall. One had a butcher knife in his fist while the other had a stake of wood. Another two wove past us brandishing stakes and jars of clear liquid at the second rabid. The creature looked between the Sentinels and the newcomers in quick evaluation and then turned tail and bolted.

"Run, y'all!" the brunette woman yelled at us.

The first rabid snarled, shoving both men back and then lunging at the nearest one, driving him into the wall with his fangs aimed at the man's throat.

Asher was already there. Disarming the human with a move so fast I couldn't even tell what he'd done before it was finished, Asher took the guy's blade, twisted it around, and slammed it into the rabid's neck.

The creature stepped back, contempt on his face. With a croaking laugh from the damage to his throat, he reached up and pulled out the butcher knife. "This isn't yours, Sentin—"

A gunshot shattered his head and his words alike.

Lowering a handgun, a woman with short-cropped gray hair and dark-brown skin threw a quick glance at the man whom the rabid had attacked. "You okay, Tyler?"

Grunting with annoyance, Tyler straightened, his ruddy face splotchy with residual anger, and Asher stepped away, putting himself between the man and us. I retreated too, trying to keep my family behind me, my whole body shaking. On the floor, the rabid's body began turning to dust. God knew no myths *I'd* ever read talked about using guns on a vampire, but clearly the myths missed the obvious.

Not much survived without a head.

I clamped my lips shut, feeling vaguely hysterical.

"You folks all right?" one of the men asked while nearby the brunette comforted the young woman and helped her gather her books from the floor.

"We're good." Mom stepped past me, though she didn't try to move beyond Asher. "I'm Captain Cortwright, Fort Briar Police Department. Thank you all for your help."

"You're a cop?" the ruddy-faced man started toward us. "Where the hell were you last night? My brother's a sergeant, and we haven't been able to reach him in—"

"Tyler." The gray-haired woman put a hand to the man's arm, a cautioning look in her brown eyes.

Mom's face tightened. "I was... in the hospital. Just got out."

"They *burned* the hospital," the brunette woman retorted.

I could read the fury and frustration on Mom's face. She might as well have said out loud that she should have been there to help. But she only replied, "We escaped."

"And who's this then?" A blond man jerked his chin at Asher. "Those were quite some moves you had there."

My heart hit my throat at the accusation in his voice and the way he still gripped the stake in his fist, and my eyes flicked to the woman with the backpack. She was watching us, and the fear in her eyes wasn't reserved for the rabid turning to dust on the floor.

If she let the other humans here know what she'd heard in the moments before they showed up...

"Asher Smith, U.S. Special Forces." Asher offered his hand, and after a heartbeat, the man shook it warily.

"Military's already here?" the man asked.

"I'm on leave. Visiting my aunt and uncle in the hospital." He nodded back toward Mom and Dad, never taking his eyes from the man. "Got them out before the fire started and came to check on my cousins and their friends."

I tried to keep from giving away any reaction to the effortless way he spun the lies. Did he and the others do this all the time? Come up with cover stories on the fly?

Probably. Nine hundred years of hiding in plain sight would certainly give them a lot of practice.

Asher continued. "What is all this?"

"Neighborhood watch," the brunette woman said, a bite in her tone. "Apocalypse edition."

"Local news is down, but stations nearby say it's folks pretending to be vampires," the blond man said. "Nothing about *pretending* here, if you ask me."

"We saw these things out last night," Tyler added. "People turning into shadows and then back, biting anyone they came across and then giving them their own damn blood."

"They took out a city bus right in front of my apartment building," the blond man continued. "Put the fucking thing right through the wall of a church and *laughed.*"

"Helen got us organized this morning," the brunette said, nodding to the woman who'd shot the rabid.

"Checking the neighborhood. Making sure people are all right. We were just starting to patrol this block when we spotted them grabbing her." She twitched her chin at the young woman with the backpack.

"You folks really should stay in your apartment," Helen said. "Get some of your household cleaners, if you've got any. Mix up some of this stuff." She gestured to the jars of liquid still clutched in several people's hands. "Jeremy here's a science teacher over at the middle school. He can give you a recipe."

Harper made a confused sound. "It's not holy water?"

Helen laughed. "I don't know about holy water, but this acid mix sure seems to do the trick."

"Just be careful," warned a nervous-looking man near the back of the group in a tone that reminded me of every teacher I'd ever had. "Wrong combination and you'll poison yourself before you can get near one of these things." He started toward us. "The right combination takes a bit of time to make, so you really should get back in—"

Asher simply shifted his weight, but it had the effect of bringing the man to a halt. "Thanks," he said. "But we have a few more folks we need to check on."

The science teacher's eyes darted between us all warily, but he backed away again.

"We oughta get out in the sunlight," Tyler said, still eyeing the Sentinels, and immediately, I knew what *had* to be the reason for his suggestion. Fastest way to prove someone wasn't a vampire.

Except when it came to us.

Asher nodded to the man, still keeping himself

between us and the newcomers. In silence, we filed down the apartment building corridor.

"I just didn't... I didn't think it was real," the young woman said to the brunette as we passed her. With shaking hands, she clutched her backpack close. "The school locked us in the library last night, but I didn't... I didn't think it was *real*."

Her eyes crept up toward us, and my heart hit my throat again. We needed to get out of here before she told the humans what the rabids said about us.

The bright sunlight made me wince, but thanks to how recently I'd fed from Ulysses, nothing else happened to me. The memory made my chest ache, though. We had to save him somehow.

Watching us like he thought maybe we'd still burst into flames, Tyler crossed his arms when we reached the parking lot behind the apartment building. For their part, the other humans were already turning their attention to scanning the surrounding area.

"If you feel like hanging around for a bit," Helen said to Asher. "We could use somebody with your skill helping with the neighborhood watch."

"Sorry," he said, and to his credit, he actually sounded it. "Need to go check on our friends."

She nodded as if she'd half expected the answer. "Be safe out there."

Murmuring our thanks, we waved as the group set off into the neighborhood again, weapons in their hands and their attention on the surrounding houses, far too many of which looked empty.

Biting my lip briefly, I hesitated when we reached Ollie's car. "You sure you're going to be okay?"

"Yeah." Ollie nodded. "We'll be fine. Stay in touch, okay?"

I nodded back.

Nervousness rolled through me as my friends climbed into the vehicle, but I buried it beneath a smile. Starting the engine, Ollie gave me a smile too before pulling her car from the parking lot.

"Come on," Asher said. "Manor. Now."

7

———————

WREN

In the front seat of the car, I clenched my hands together and tried not to flinch every time a gunshot rang out. We'd seen more neighborhood watch groups patrolling the streets as we drove through town— ragtag clusters of people clutching whatever weapons they could find, checking on their neighbors but also jumping and shouting at any shadow that happened to move. That most vampires couldn't survive daylight surely must have occurred to some of them by now.

Though maybe there were more of the rabids like we'd run into spreading throughout town, using leather and darkened glass to get around the fact they shouldn't have been able to be out in the sun without dying.

Another gunshot made me jump, and my eyes snapped around, searching for the source of the sound before I spotted a big guy with a stained t-shirt stretched over his belly, waving a gun and shouting at a tree shadow that maybe had just moved with the breeze. In his other hand, he clutched a beer can. With a flourish like a drunken Wild West gunslinger, he fired at the ground again as if to kill the shadow.

"Dammit," Mom whispered in the back seat. The need to get out of the car and intervene practically radiated from her. In the driver's seat, Liam's jaw muscles jumped, but he didn't slow down.

"We have to get the girls somewhere safe," Dad murmured, and when I turned around, I saw him put a hand to Mom's, trying to calm her like he always seemed to be able to do. Frustration still seethed in her expression, but after a heartbeat, she managed a nod.

In silence, we drove onward. Fire crews sped past us, still attending to the various blazes burning around town, though we passed several of their trucks that'd been toppled over like maybe rabids had gotten to them before the sun rose. Meanwhile, tow trucks were busy trying to extract vehicles from buildings where the rabids had thrown them. But we hadn't spotted many cops, if any, and my stomach twisted at the memory of what we'd seen of the police station.

Pollen, pollen carries the bumblebee...

I shuddered. I didn't know what the hell the rabid meant, but it had to just be some kind of mind game. Maybe an old poem Asher or Liam would know, and they could explain what he'd been implying.

While looking right at me.

I shoved the thought aside. It wouldn't mean anything.

Except there'd been that dormant...

And wherever she goes, she sets us free.

My fingers clenched tighter on each other. When

she'd run up to Asher, the woman had been okay. She'd been asking for help with the rabids. And then she'd looked at me, and the boy with her had too, and suddenly they weren't okay anymore at all.

And as for what happened at the clinic...

His missing piece.

A rough breath left me, and I released my hands only to dig my fingernails into the armrest beside me, hanging onto anything real. This couldn't be because of *me*. I'd heard that voice in my head too, same as it seemed like everyone else had, and I'd burned him out. Sure, I didn't know *how* I'd done that, or even what happened in the first place, but...

What other vampires had I seen since getting away from Priscilla and the rabids, back when they held me prisoner in Cincinnati?

I trembled. None. None besides the Sentinels, anyway. The vampires at the clinic were the first.

God, I couldn't breathe, and the fact I technically didn't need to wasn't doing jack for how I felt like my head was spinning.

The town fell behind us, and after a while, the forest closed in around the car. It wasn't until the trees shut away the view of smoke that still rose from the city that I was finally able to release my death-grip on the armrest. Like I could finally focus on something besides the destruction.

Because in the midst of all this, racing back to a magical manor occupied by demons had somehow become a relief.

At the last turn ahead of us, Asher's motorcycle slowed. Liam eased off the gas to avoid hitting him.

I glanced between them, confused. "What is it?"

Saying nothing, Liam brought the car to a stop. Pushing open the door, he climbed out.

An acrid stench clung to the air.

Oh, dear God. I scrambled out after him. It had to just be the smoke carrying from the city. Barnaby and Friday had layers upon layers of protection around the manor, rendering it basically invisible and unfindable to anyone who didn't know it was there. Even *satellites* couldn't see this place.

I rounded the turn, and a tiny gasp escaped me.

In the clearing where the manor stood, nothing but burned rubble and stone remained, torn down like a child destroying a construction of building blocks. Charred timbers stuck up like insect legs from the wreckage, and shattered glass glinted in the sunlight.

"It's an illusion," I whispered. Dragging my gaze to Asher and Liam, I gave them a desperate look. "Like when they made it look like a farmhouse outside and a manor inside."

Asher glanced at Liam, who nodded and walked forward into the clearing.

No defenses lashed out. Nothing in the air shimmered to alter what we saw.

Carefully, Liam started into the debris, moving gingerly like he expected lingering protections around the place to strike out at him. But nothing changed, and after a moment, he bent down, pulling something from the wreckage.

I pressed my knuckles to my mouth at the sight of Friday's white apron, now splattered with blood.

"Is she dead?" Harper called, her voice unsteady.

Liam looked around and then signed to Asher.

"Nothing else here," Asher translated.

I made myself keep breathing. The demons were thousands of years old. They were terrifyingly powerful. So maybe this was a trick. Maybe they'd done this because they saw what was happening with the vampires, and they'd decided to run and...

And abandon the Sentinels?

Friday and Barnaby would never. I'd only met them a few times, but I knew they felt like they owed the guys. Moreover, they really seemed to care about them, acting like equal parts polite servants and doting grandparents. The last thing they'd do would be to leave without telling the Sentinels where they'd gone.

"So..." Dad started. "Those rabid things did this?"

"How did they even know it was *here*?" Harper looked around like maybe the trees or the sky could give us the answer. "We could barely even find this place the other day."

My stomach turned into a ball of lead. Oh, God, no. No, no, no. Amalie had known where to send those rabids to find Ollie and Emma, maybe because of me. And now...

"Your friends," Mom said.

I looked over at her in confusion. She was watching the Sentinels.

"The two that are missing," she continued.

My head shook. "Ulysses and Gideon wouldn't tell anyone how to find this place."

Her mouth tightened, and the pit in my stomach deepened. Was I sure of that? All things being equal, yeah, I could definitely say those two wouldn't give a homicidal maniac directions to find the demons.

But whatever happened to the other vampires at the clinic had been starting to take Ulysses too. And that rabid said he and Gideon were *feasting* now.

I closed my eyes. Was I arguing that this might be Ulysses' or Gideon's fault just to make myself feel better? God, I hoped not. But either this *was* my fault or the Sentinels—or maybe something else entirely I hadn't even thought of.

Amalie could be torturing them.

I shook my head at the wreckage as if it were arguing with me. The Sentinels had survived centuries with her. They wouldn't break under torture.

What if this was me?

What if it *all* was?

My mind spinning, I retreated from the others, circling wide around the destroyed manor. Glass and burnt wood crunched under my feet, and the smell of smoke wasn't the only thing making my eyes sting. I felt like my body was radiating poison. Like someone had opened a window in my skull, putting everything important to me on display. I'd swear on every holy book I could find that Amalie wasn't in my mind. Not anymore. She'd left me for dead, for God's sake. But what else could she be destroying now, thanks to the time she *had* spent in my head? Yeah, it'd let me see her past, but apparently it had also given her a peek into mine.

Which meant I'd possibly cost those nice demons their lives.

My eyes crept over to my family, and my heart began

to pound harder, air entering and leaving my chest in rapid gasps. Anywhere we went, anything we did that might even *kind of* be something I'd think of or remember, and Amalie could think of it too.

And if I came near any vampires...

The ground felt unsteady beneath my feet. Debris crunched nearby, and I looked up to see Asher walking toward me. I retreated farther, shaking my head. "I'm so sorry," I whispered, holding up a hand to keep him back. "It's my fault. She saw my memories and—"

"It's *her* fault, Wren. Not yours."

"But she—"

"Is the monster. Not you."

I stared at him. How could he be sure of that?

"But..." My whole body was shaking so damn hard. "What that rabid said..." A sob tried to escape me, and my lips clamped shut for a moment as I fought to keep it inside. "They must have done something when they kidnapped me. It's the only explanation. That dormant was okay till she met me. And now—"

"Wren," Harper said, and my eyes snapped over. She walked toward me, both caution and concern on her face, and my mouth moved, but I couldn't figure out what to say to her. I'd possibly gotten our only chance at safety destroyed.

And if anyone stayed with me, they'd be in danger now too.

Cold pain settled inside my chest like my lungs were sharing space with a shard of ice, and I couldn't hope to breathe around it. That was the answer, though, wasn't it?

I had to leave.

"Asher." I cleared my throat, trying to make my voice steadier than it'd been. "I need you to take my family, and—"

"No."

"*Please.* I need you to—"

"I'm not leaving you. And neither will Liam. So we need a new plan."

Desperation made me want to scream. "But—"

"No."

"Dammit, you *have* to."

"Like hell."

His expression was like iron, and I turned away, raking my hands through my hair. Damn him, I couldn't stay. Didn't he understand that? I could be endangering him too.

I'd never risk that. Never.

Asher's hand took my arm, and I couldn't summon up the energy to resist when he pulled me around to face him. But I couldn't bring myself to meet his eyes.

"We aren't going to abandon you," he murmured so quietly I doubted anyone else could hear. "Not now. Not ever."

A warm, pained feeling lodged in my chest, but it wasn't helping anything. I couldn't stay with my family. The Sentinels wouldn't leave without me. And that...

Left Harper.

My eyes found my sister again, and the gray look on her face was enough to let me know she'd figured out the direction my thoughts had taken. Her head shook, resistance on her face, and it propelled me toward her.

"You're our only option," I said to her silently protesting expression.

"We stick together. We always—"

"Not this time."

Mom started toward us. "Wren, what are you saying?"

My insides quaked. I didn't want to argue with them. I wanted them to run away and keep going so Amalie couldn't ever use me to find them—and, God, that hurt.

"I need you to go," I said. "This is me. My fault." I held up a hand when Asher started to argue. "There's a strong chance Amalie saw the manor in my mind, and that's why she was able to find it. Find Ollie and Emma too. And if that's true, then you're in danger if you stay with me."

Mom's head shook. "We're not leaving you alone in this madness!"

"There's no other choice. You have to stay safe, and I can't—"

"Wren, *none* of this is safe, and I won't have my daughter out in the middle of it where I can't help her!"

The warm ache in my chest grew stronger, throbbing inside me like gratitude that hurt because things couldn't actually be the way she said. From a few feet away, Dad watched us all, his expression displeased.

"I have to help *you*," I told them. "All of you. You heard that rabid back at the apartment. Amalie is hunting me. And that means we *can't* stay together, because then none of you will be safe."

"I won't just drive off and leave you alone while you're—"

"She won't be alone," Asher said.

A ragged breath left my mother as she turned to him.

"I'm sorry, but we don't know you. I appreciate all you did for my daughters, but—"

"They're centuries-old vampires, Mom, and everything in their world is scared to cross them."

"And we'll protect your daughter with our lives," Asher said. "I swear to you."

I turned back to him, a protest on my lips because like hell they'd *die* for me.

He didn't take his eyes from my parents.

"I'm supposed to just take your word for that?" my mother countered. "No, we stick together. I appreciate how you've helped us"—she made a conciliatory gesture to Asher—"but we need to get back in that car *together* and find another option here."

"Mom, please! I can't lose you, okay? I *can't*."

"And we can't lose you!"

I looked away. I didn't know what else to do. Friday and Barnaby had been my safest bet, and, God, what Amalie had done...

Nausea churned in me. "You have to go," I said to my family again. "Please."

"No!" Mom retorted. "We're not splitting up just because a bunch of goddamn *vampires* are—"

"How will this keep you safer, Wren?" Dad interrupted quietly.

I hesitated. "Because then I won't have to worry about you. If Amalie comes anywhere near me, I can just run." I shivered. "And she can't use you against me."

Dad looked away, a thoughtful expression on his face.

"You aren't seriously *considering* this?" Mom protested incredulously.

"I think things are a bit beyond our control right now, and if our presence actually endangers her..."

Mom faltered, her angry expression cracking into desperation. Her mouth moved, and I could see so many of her counterarguments rising and falling without ever making it into the air.

"But how will we know you're okay?" Harper asked in a small voice.

"I-I don't know. You can't go anywhere I might think of. If Amalie knows everything I know, then—"

"You can call me." Asher rattled off a number. "When you get somewhere safe, you leave a message on that line, and we'll get it."

Silence fell, and I didn't know how to break it. Or even if I wanted to.

I had to run. And so did they.

Mom muttered a curse under her breath and looked over at me. "We're going to see you again soon. You understand?"

I nodded quickly.

Her eyes darted across Asher and Liam, and her mouth compressed, but she didn't say anything else. Dad pulled me into a hug, squeezing me tightly. "Soon," he echoed, his voice muffled.

Tears stung my eyes. I didn't know how else to keep them safe, but God, I felt like my heart was being ripped out.

He released me, and then Harper was there. For a moment, my sister just stood in front of me, and then she engulfed me in a hug so tight, it was like she was trying to squeeze every ounce of her love into my body.

"We'll be okay," she said. "So you have to be okay too, got it?"

I nodded against her shoulder.

Another second passed before she let me go, holding me out at arm's length. "Love you."

I nodded again. "Love you," I repeated, my voice thick.

She tried for a smile, but the expression was fractured.

Mom stepped closer and pulled me to her. "You be so careful, you understand? So, *so* careful. And you use that sword thing and you stab the hell out of anything that threatens you."

I choked on a laugh, but it couldn't last long against the tears burning my eyes. I nodded fast.

With Harper and Dad, she headed for the car.

Pain like I'd been the one stabbed ached in my gut. I had to believe I'd see them again, and that this was the best option. Amalie was hunting me and the Sentinels. Keeping my family anywhere near me wasn't a good idea.

They opened the car doors and then looked back.

"Love you, sweetheart," Dad called.

Struggle showed on my mom's face, as if she was still trying to find a way to argue this. But her eyes were fierce when she looked at me. "Love you, Wren," she said like she was trying to burn the words into me.

Harper gave me a pained smile.

"Love you all too." My voice was choked.

They climbed into the sedan, and I choked on a sob as they drove away.

8

ASHER

Gods, I wished I could've spared Wren this pain. Agony practically radiated from her as she stood frozen, watching the path her family had taken long after their car was gone. Her love for them was so fierce, and her strength too. Sending them away when clearly it was ripping her heart out to do it...

My heart ached for her. Before I became a vampire, I'd had no family. I'd been just another orphan of war, found by soldiers and raised by them from the time I was four years old—though it could scarcely be called *raising*. Scrambling along with all the other children in the camp, I fought to eat, to sleep, to live. Until I became one of the Sentinels, I'd barely had a connection close enough to be called a friend, let alone a parent or sibling.

But Wren obviously did, and a simple phone number to tell us they were safe felt like nothing compared to the protection I wished I could give them—for her sake, on top of just being the right thing to do. Just as bad was how

Wren obviously blamed herself for all this, even though there was zero reason she should.

That rabid was full of shit as far as I was concerned, and his little poem was too. *Wren* wasn't changing the dormants into rabids. And Ulysses or Gideon could have led Amalie to the demons. The mere suggestion felt impossible, but I couldn't discount how Ulysses had suddenly radiated the same *wrongness* as a rabid at the clinic. Add to that how, since he and Gideon had been captured, I hadn't felt a trace of the connection to them that had defined our lives for centuries, and the fault for this situation could lie with either of them.

Shivers crawled over my skin as I searched for my link to them again instinctively, but nothing had changed. The connection to them was just *gone*. If they were dead, the backlash of that bond breaking should have killed us too. That's what Amalie always told us.

So either she lied... or something else had happened.

My eyes slid to the ruins of the manor. Liam had started picking his way through the destruction again, searching for clues. But the debris field was huge, and most of it was locked in some intermediate stage between the manor it had been and the farmhouse it had pretended to be, like the magics had crashed into each other when the place came down. A chunk of marble staircase turned to rotted wooden steps midway down, and a blue tarp half covered a crystal chandelier. Tendrils of smoke drifted up from scattered mounds of granite and wood. And the idea that Amalie had grown *this* strong in only—what?—*days*? It was mind-boggling.

Of course, this might have been Urlfeige instead.

Chills rolled through me, like that ancient monster was hovering behind my shoulder, laughing at us. I glanced over at the others and opted for sign language rather than risk saying something that would make this all worse for Wren.

Anything? I asked Liam.

He shook his head. *No trace of the demons. More blood to the west. Whatever happened, it might have started over there.* He paused. *They could have run.*

I met his eyes. Neither of us believed that.

Grimacing, I scanned the forest around us. Her family had taken the only car, which of course made sense, but we couldn't all of us ride the motorcycle. *Garage might still be—*

The sound of helicopter blades chopping the air carried over the forest.

Adrenaline shot through me. There wasn't time to grab the bike, not with how fast those things were closing in.

I ran for Wren. Snagging her arm, I raced for the shelter of the forest, Liam right behind me.

Black helicopters swept over the clearing only a moment after we made it beneath the trees.

Banking hard, they circled back again immediately, coming to hover over the ruins of the manor. "Fuck," I muttered.

"GSS?" Wren whispered.

"Probably."

I didn't elaborate. It might be the slayers, but the gods knew the Consortium would be on their way too. The politicians who oversaw much of the supernatural world loved to hide behind their red tape, hold debates, and generally take their sweet time on everything. But an entire clinic and town inexplicably going rabid? Yeah, that'd get their attention.

Regardless, if these people had stopped—hell, if they saw this place at all—then the protection on the clearing must be gone entirely.

They'd be down here any second.

Doors slid open on the sides of the helicopters like the bastards had heard my thoughts.

"Come on." Shifting my grip from her arm to her hand, I eased back into the woods, avoiding sudden movements that might draw their eyes. The garage was tucked away in the forest, and the path to it was on the opposite end of the clearing. There was no way we could circle this open space anywhere close to where they might see.

Long way 'round it was.

Without a word, Liam moved behind us, guarding our backs as we retreated farther into the woods.

A commanding voice carried from the clearing. "Team One, north quadrant. Team Two, south. Find the girl."

Shit.

Wren's hand clenched down on mine, but she didn't make a sound as I sped up, weaving through the undergrowth as fast as staying silent would let me. My free hand itched to summon my knife, but that wouldn't help yet and might just draw attention too.

The clearing fell farther behind us. I kept heading away from it, not willing to circle back right away. The smell of wet moss and stone began to carry on the air, and the sound of running water followed. The terrain gradually began to descend, becoming more uneven, full of rocks overgrown with lichen and holes waiting to catch our feet.

I frowned, thinking fast. It'd been a while since I'd explored much of the woods around the manor. With the demons' magic, humans weren't a threat and there was little chance of rabids nearby, so there just hadn't been as much need to monitor it.

But if I remembered correctly...

The woods gave way to cliff walls carved into the terrain by the rivulet of water running past. It wasn't the river—that was miles away—but it was a tributary of it, and in thunderstorms, the runoff made this place impassable.

And right now, it'd cover our trail if whoever brought those helicopters had brought any shifters too.

"Stick close to the walls," I whispered to Wren. "Out of view as much as you can. But follow when I head for the water, okay?"

She nodded quickly.

My eyes met Liam's briefly. He nodded once.

If anything threatened us, he'd make sure it died fast.

Gripping her hand, I crept along the base of the cliff wall. Stone outcroppings sheltered us, as did the trees clinging to their edges, casting green shadows down on the limestone and gravel. Water stains coated the walls, marking them black and green with edges of blue in a few places. And all along this stretch, there were a few small caves that could give us a place to retreat if anyone—

Gravel clattered up ahead.

Liam was past us in an instant, his knife already in his fist.

A panicked cry followed. Outside one of the caves up ahead, Liam stopped. After a heartbeat, his knife vanished and he held up a hand like he was trying to reassure someone.

My brow twitched down, but I didn't make a sound as I waited for him to explain.

Not taking his eyes from whatever he saw, he motioned for me to come closer. With a twitch of my head to tell Wren to stay back by the cliff wall, I walked toward him and peered around the opening.

A young couple huddled at the very back of the small cave, just beyond the reach of the sun. The man had light-brown skin and dark hair, and the woman was so pale, redheaded, and freckled, I'd be shocked if she hadn't come from Ireland. The sleeve of the man's sweater was torn, and fangs were retreating between the woman's lips, the reaction more instinctive than threatening if her expression was any indication. Neither of them could have been more than twenty-five when they were turned, and their eyes were still young enough that it probably hadn't been that long ago either. With their arms around each other, they stared at me and Liam like we were their salvation.

"Sentinels?" the man asked.

I nodded. "What are you doing here?"

"Rabids," he said. "They attacked the vampire neighborhood in Fort Briar. They were dragging people out of their homes, saying it was time to be free." A tremor went through him. "We tried to help our neighbors, but..."

"They killed them," the woman finished, her voice shaking and her Irish accent thick. "Almost killed us too. Because they said we weren't 'seeing the truth' like we should. And then when we spotted the fires in town..."

The guy pulled her closer, comforting her.

I couldn't show my own horror at what they described. It'd only scare them. "I'm sorry. We just came from there."

"Is anyone still alive?" the man asked, something in his tone like he was bracing himself for the answer.

I weighed how to respond. "Yes, but something's happened to them. You need to stay away."

"But—"

"The GSS or the Consortium are in these woods. Keep quiet until sunset and then get as far from here as you can. Understand?"

The man nodded, his arm tightening around the woman.

I nodded back, wishing there was more I could do for them. But the sunlight would kill them and we couldn't stay, not with people after Wren.

With a nod to Liam, I started past the cave.

A choked cry came from the woman. My attention snapped back.

She was staring at Wren.

Apprehension prickled through me like a wave of needles. With a choked gasp, Wren retreated behind the cliff wall again, but it didn't matter. The horror on the couple's faces deepened with every passing second.

"No," the woman gasped. "No, please. She... oh, God."

The man grunted, cringing in on himself, one hand clutching his head.

My knife appeared in my hand, though I barely noticed myself summoning it.

This was *not* possible.

"He... he's in my head." The woman stumbled to her feet, lurching forward like she was being pulled toward Wren, only to retreat when she neared the lighter shadows cast by the sun. "I hear... He's..." She shuddered hard, a mad grin starting to twitch on her lips like something else was taking control of her face.

The man's eyes snapped up. There was nothing sane left in his gaze.

And everything about him radiated the wrongness of a rabid.

The guy surged to his feet, lunging toward where Wren hid outside the cave, her back pressed to the cliff wall and her chest rising and falling in panicked breaths. I moved fast, blocking his path immediately, but the man stopped shy of the sunlight. As he stared toward where she hid, his teeth pulled back from his fangs in a savage grin. "He wants you, girl. You free us."

Oh, no *fucking* way.

I grabbed Wren and took off running, Liam on my heels, while behind us, the young couple shrieked, trapped by the sun.

9

WREN

I t was me.

Oh, God, it really *was* me doing this, even if I had no clue how.

I didn't know whether to cry or scream.

But I didn't think I'd ever forget the shrieks coming from the cave behind us.

Feeling like ice had replaced my blood, I ran behind Asher along the base of the cliff wall. His grip on my hand was like iron and determination radiated from him, as if he'd sooner burn the world than let me go. Liam was behind me, his swift footsteps barely making a sound on the gravel and his expression deadly as hell.

But those people had been fine. Really, truly fine.

Until they just *looked* at me.

"This way," Asher said. Veering left, he started up a steep trail out of the ravine. I climbed after him, grabbing at the rocks and roots to stabilize myself.

But I didn't want to be here. What if whatever was happening was simply delayed for the guys, and any moment now, it would start to hurt Asher and Liam too?

We reached the top of the ravine, and Asher took off through the woods, never slowing down. If anyone had heard those shrieks—and who couldn't? Even here, they were echoing in my ears—then they'd be after us.

After me.

I scrambled over a fallen log, my hand slipping on the moss clinging to the rotting wood. I couldn't stay with the guys. With *anyone.* I needed to find a hole and fucking bury myself in it, if that's what it took to keep people safe.

Should I just shift my shape and fly away from the Sentinels?

Guilt colored the thought, even though it was practical. They couldn't fly now. Something had happened to them to stop that. So it'd be easy, even if I remembered hearing that flying as a shadow in the sun was draining at best. It'd probably hurt like hell too.

Not as much as endangering them did.

Leaving would protect them. Protect everyone. That was the most important—

Asher stopped suddenly, and I nearly barreled into him before I could stop too. Looking around fast, I couldn't see what had made him pause.

Helicopter blades chopped the air somewhere in the distance.

I could head for those.

Except if that was the GSS, they'd probably kill me.

I stared up at the blue sky beyond the treetops, and I

shivered. I wasn't suicidal, but God help me, I had to protect the Sentinels. The only two who weren't captives of Amalie, anyway… and how much longer would *that* last if they were anywhere near me?

You free us.

The shivers grew worse. I couldn't stay.

Asher glanced over his shoulder at me, and I realized I'd been pulling my hand from his. I faltered at the look in his eyes. Determined and cautious and questioning all at the same time.

The chopping noise grew louder. Any moment now, the helicopter would be visible past the tops of the autumn trees.

My body quivered. It'd be easy. Painful in *so* many ways, but I could shift and go and everybody would be safe.

Liam appeared at the corner of my eye, and my attention snapped over to him. He wasn't touching me, wasn't doing more than watching me in the shadows of the foliage.

His head shook ever so slightly, a plea in his gaze.

Tears stung my eyes. I couldn't risk them. Couldn't lose them. Not to this and not ever.

"Don't, Wren," Asher whispered. "Please."

I looked up at the brilliant blue sky, my heart breaking.

The helicopter faded into the distance.

Asher's hand tightened on mine. Gently, he pulled me closer, wrapping his arm around me and holding me to his chest. "You and I have been far closer than this since you escaped the rabids," he whispered. "And I'm still okay. Whatever is happening, we'll fix it together."

I squeezed my eyes shut, wanting to argue. Yes, we'd slept together, but I'd also fed from Ulysses and now he was rabid too. What if I made that happen?

Though, Ulysses said Amalie had his knife, right before whatever this was took him over.

I buried my head in Asher's shoulder, trembling at my fears and all the unknowns.

"We'll fix it," he repeated. "But right now, we have to run."

I nodded against his jacket.

Tension seeped from him like he'd been bracing himself to see if I'd agree. Taking my hand again, he drew me with him as we started off into the forest again. Weaving through the trees on a path I couldn't see, we continued on until finally, a small brick building came into view.

I glanced at Asher, surprised. It looked like a little single-car garage.

At the edge of the tree line, he paused, scanning the surrounding area like he was searching for traps before moving forward again. I studied the garage as we came closer. The bricks were pockmarked with age and moss grew in the gaps. The door was covered in dents and rust. The whole place gave the impression of having been abandoned for years, but I knew that, when it came to demons, that didn't mean much.

Especially since everything in me wanted to head away from this place right now, and even when I glanced at the forest around the building, my eyes wanted to go anywhere else.

Just like the manor before it'd been destroyed.

Carefully, Asher inched closer to the building, watching around him like he was keeping an eye out for traps. Gripping the handle, he eased the garage open, and despite its coating of rust, the door didn't make a single sound.

A little empty garage lay beyond the opening, with nothing but spiderwebs clinging to the ceiling and a dented gas can lying on the concrete floor.

"Come on." Asher drew me with him into the garage.

I winced, my vision warping like I was walking through carnival glass, and suddenly, the little room wasn't so little anymore. Instead, a dark space stretched ahead of us, cavernous. Dozens of vehicles were arrayed along the expansive concrete—sports cars and army surplus vehicles and SUVs. Even motorcycles in a row.

Keeping me with him, Asher headed farther inside. Behind us, Liam tugged the garage door closed again. Lights flickered on overhead, illuminating the rows nearest to us.

"They really do love that 'bigger on the inside' trick, don't they?" I murmured.

Asher chuckled. "Barnaby's collected cars since they were created. Says the internal combustion engine reminds him of something Hell might've invented." A grimace crossed his face. "Or..."

Present tense, I realized. He'd said it like the demon was still alive.

"They could still be out there," I offered.

He nodded, but I could tell from his face he didn't believe it. "This way."

Heading left, he led me past rows of sports cars in every shade of the rainbow. Unlike any other garage I'd ever been inside, the smell of rubber and oil was only barely detectable. The air was cool and had a quality like we were inside a cave, not walking deeper into the warehouse of a demon's car collection.

Though maybe it was both. What did I know about how they made this place?

Leaving the sports cars behind, Asher continued on until he reached a large black SUV that looked like it could withstand the apocalypse itself.

Which seemed good, even if it wasn't exactly subtle.

"So where are we going?" I asked.

His mouth tightened. "Not sure. We can't risk anywhere Ulysses or Gideon would know."

"Or me."

He didn't respond. Taking out his cell, he thumbed it on and then clicked a few icons before lifting it to his ear.

The person on the other end picked up on the first ring. "If this is some rabid bullshit, I will end you."

I tensed at the threat, looking to Asher in alarm, but he only said, "Hey, Laz."

Silence hung for a moment. I glanced around uncomfortably, uncertain whether I should pull my hand from Asher's and retreat to where I couldn't overhear his call.

"You still you?" demanded the gruff man on the other end.

"Yep."

More silence.

"Consortium's got a bug up their ass over Fort Briar, and the GSS is crawling all over the town," the guy said finally. "This shit your doing?"

"No. But we need your help."

A scoff followed.

"We need somewhere safe to stay. Off the grid." Asher paused. "Way off."

For a long moment, the other man didn't respond. "How bad is it?"

"Amalie's back. She took out a house built by demons. And she has Ulysses and Gideon."

The guy whistled. "You need another *planet*, kid."

"No kidding."

Discomfort finally won out. Extracting my hand, I retreated to the SUV, joining Liam where he leaned against it.

"Not a problem," Asher said to the man on the phone.

I dropped my gaze to the cement floor rather than look at Liam. I didn't have a clue what to say to him. All of this, everything that'd happened... it was all because of me, and nothing I could do would make it any better.

Liam's hand brushed my forearm.

My breath caught at the contact. I glanced up at him.

His fingers strayed down to the back of my hand before ghosting away, and he gave me a small smile. "Not your fault," he said, his rasping voice a whisper.

My heart ached.

"Thanks, Laz." Asher hung up the phone and came toward us. "We've got a place."

Liam turned, pulling open the rear passenger door of the SUV and then motioning for me to climb in. Leather creaked under me as I got inside, and new-car smell clung to the air.

The back hatch of the SUV opened. Asher pushed it up and out of his way, his eyes on the spare tire panel in the floor. Twisting in the seat, I watched as he pulled it aside.

There was no tire. Instead, a collection of duffel bags were stuffed inside.

"Liam." He drew out one of them, handing it to the other man without another word. His face tightened as he pulled two others out of the way, setting them aside, and then he paused as two more bags came into view.

His eyes flicked up to me.

"What?" I asked.

He hefted one of them up and offered it to me. Warily, I took it.

Clothes for me were inside. A hairbrush and tooth-brush and even shampoo and conditioner as well. A case of those snack cube things was tucked at the bottom, in case I couldn't feed and needed to stay alive.

I looked back up at Asher. He had a sad smile on his face.

"Like they knew you'd stay with us," he murmured. Shaking his head, he grabbed the last bag and then shut the panel, leaving the other two in the back.

Because they were Ulysses' and Gideon's, I realized. And all of them were supplies made by the demons for each of the Sentinels, in case they needed to escape this way.

And for me.

Asher circled the vehicle and climbed into the driver's

seat. As Liam got in too, Asher turned the key that I wasn't really surprised was already in the ignition.

The engine growled to life.

A breath left me as he guided the vehicle from the garage. I had no idea where we were going or what was going to happen now, but thanks to the demons who were *hopefully* still out there somewhere, we were as ready as we'd ever be.

10

GIDEON

They'd moved me five times, and now I'd lost any way of knowing where I was, not that I'd been certain before. But every time they relocated me, they put a bag over my head and kept the shackles on my arms while at least eight of them dragged me from the room to a vehicle and then back into another room again, where I was chained to yet another wall.

And left waiting.

Breathing slowly, I focused on staying calm. They hadn't taken the bag from my head this time, which meant I was effectively blind to the room around me—a fact that left nascent panic thrumming like electrical surges through my veins. Was it on purpose? Likely. Just another of Amalie's games, tormenting me with the feeling of being blinded.

Or else the rabids were lazy.

I drew another breath through my nose and released it from my mouth, attempting to focus on my other senses.

There weren't many sounds, at least not close by. Voices, but muffled as if they were far away beyond closed doors or long halls. The ground was still beneath my feet, carrying no reverberations of footsteps. Better construction than the place where my captivity had begun, then. The walls certainly felt more solid, as if they truly were stone. But I could only smell the musty stench of the bag over my head, and there was no point in tasting the damn thing.

Thus endeth the inventory of my other senses, barring the fact my heart was pounding like a kettledrum.

I squeezed my eye shut. I wasn't blind, and I wouldn't be a child afraid of the dark. Objectively, I knew it was my captivity that was making me react in this fashion. Simply being blindfolded had never sent me into a state of panic in all the years since we'd been set free of Amalie. No, it was the fact she was here, and alive, and now I could not see that tormented me, bringing back countless memories of the games she used to play. The ones where I never knew if I'd make it out of the room with my remaining eye intact.

My heart beat harder. Damn me. Thinking about the past wasn't helping anything.

Breathing as steadily as I could, I attempted to stretch out my mind, searching again for my connection to the other Sentinels, even if I hadn't been able to find anything of them so far. Distance impacted the strength of our sense of each other, of course, just as proximity made it all the more intense. I wouldn't feel much of them, if anything, if they were in another city or state—or gods, country?

No, we hadn't taken planes or boats. At worst, I was in Canada or Mexico. Hardly the other side of the world.

But regardless, nothing responded to my questing thoughts. For all these centuries, I'd never particularly needed to *try* in order to feel the others. They were simply *there*. But now the horizon of my mind felt dark, as if the world simply ended where the others had once been. I could scarcely remember what it'd been like *not* to have them bound to me, and after so long, I found I didn't like this feeling in the least.

The horizon pushed back against my mind.

I winced. What the hell? That wasn't—

To my right, a door opened, and my eye snapped toward the sound.

A familiar chuckle followed, making my skin crawl. "Really, children. Leaving the poor man blind. How cruel."

Rage rolled through me at the teasing tone of Amalie's voice. But wariness joined it soon after as my nose detected the scent of blood past the musty hood over my head.

"Do take that off him, would you? It's not like we need to torture him. He'll understand us soon enough."

My wariness grew.

The hood whipped away from my face, and I winced at the sudden light. My vision cleared, affording me the sight of Amalie standing before me, a grin on her red lips and blood dripping from her hands. Six rabids stood behind her.

"Would you like a taste?" She lifted a hand to me. "It's oh so delicious."

I recoiled, but she only chuckled again. Stepping forward, she drew her fingers across my lips, smearing the blood on me as I tried to turn my face away. The scent of it assaulted my nostrils. Human. Maybe some shifter too.

Gods, how many had they killed?

"Now, Gideon, I know you've got to be hungry. Or you will be soon. But regardless, you need to keep up your strength. He's quite overwhelming when you first meet him."

My attention snapped back to her.

She smiled. "Bring him."

Two of the rabids moved toward me, and nausea roiled in my gut when I recognized them as a married dormant couple who'd lived in Fort Briar. The two men looked savage now, every trace of warmth or friendliness lost beneath a crazed look in their eyes. In their hands, they held chains and something that looked like a metal collar.

I recoiled against the wall in spite of myself. That Amalie enjoyed collaring us like animals was nothing new. But it never entailed anything good.

"Now, don't struggle, Gideon." She drew Ulysses' blade from her skirt, and her eyes slid to the other vampires around her as she smiled. "I wouldn't want to make someone suffer for your obstinance."

Yes, she would.

Gritting my teeth, I made myself remain still as the two vampires secured the collar around my neck, the metal cold and heavy against my skin. While one of the men held the chain like a leash, the other unfastened my wrists from the wall and then bound them before me with thick shackles. Grinning, the first man stepped back while his husband pulled me forward by my neck.

"This way." Amalie tucked the knife back into her skirt, though I knew it would be the work of an instant for her to bring it back out.

Ever quick with a blade, that one.

The men hauled me forward while the other rabids surrounded me, weapons drawn. Without another option, I walked forward. The room fell behind us as we passed through the metal double doors, and the corridor beyond was as stark as the space I'd just left. Nothing but cinderblock walls, concrete floor, glaring industrial lights, and not a single hint to tell me where I was. Amalie continued along the hallway, ignoring the closed doors that lined either side except for when a scream came from within.

Every time that happened, she'd throw a grin back at me as if in anticipation.

The hall turned several times, and still the rabids continued on until at last we reached a larger set of double doors with two more vampires standing outside. At the sight of Amalie, they bowed their heads and then moved quickly to push the doors open.

With effort, I kept any expression from my face at what lay inside, but it looked like the place in which a comic book villain would be created. Catwalks criss-crossed above me. Pipes ran everywhere—writhing across the distant ceiling, continuing down into the floor—all tangling around one another as if assembled by a madman. Steam seeped from several, obscuring the depths of the enormous room and lending an ominous air to the cavernous space. Enormous tanks with signs for hazardous materials stood like silent giants at intervals, and warnings were stenciled on the cement floor around them, cautioning everyone to stay away unless authorized.

Not that the rabids were paying that much attention.

At the center of the room, an enormous metal vat stood like an aboveground swimming pool made of solid metal. The contents had to be blood, given how much of it I could smell on the air, and on all sides the rabids were dropping things into it.

My eye widened as we came closer, and my feet stopped of their own accord. Not simply *things*. Severed limbs. Organs. Heads.

Dear gods, what *was* this?

The dark liquid didn't react, however, remaining eerily still as it swallowed down the sacrifices without so much as a ripple. The air pressed against my skin, so heavily laden with magic it felt like the power was trying to force its way inside my body.

I didn't even want to breathe, if only to keep this out of me.

"Isn't it marvelous?" Amalie turned, her arms spread wide.

"What hellish magic is this?" I demanded.

She laughed at me. "The rebirth of our greatness, and the return to the way things *should* have been all along."

On either side of me, the rabids tried to push me forward. I resisted, not allowing them to shove me a millimeter closer while my eyes never left the massive vat of blood. "Urlfeige," I stated.

"Yes. The original vampire. The greatest of us."

My skin crawled.

"It's taken millennia, but he will finally be restored. The vampire god and king, walking the earth once again."

The reverence in Amalie's voice tore my eyes from the blood. She'd sounded rapturous before, usually while torturing one of us, but I'd never known her to have religion or to worship anything besides herself.

"Can you feel it, Gideon?" Her eyes practically glowed. "The empty realms, only inches from our fingertips. The *power* of those beings who linger in the dark spaces between universes. They thought to make him their slave, and yet he draws on them instead. With their strength, he's survived far beyond every other vampire in the world, even beyond all his enemies did to try to destroy him."

Shivers rolled through my insides. The empty realms? Those were a legend—and not a good one. Part magic, part quantum physics, they were purported to be the buffer zone around reality itself, protecting it and preventing it from crashing into whatever lay beyond this universe. Stories told of ravenous beings who lived in that barren space, though *living* might be an overstatement. They loathed reality and existence, and yet they wanted to possess it. To encounter them was supposedly so horrible, death would be a preferable alternative.

And this thing was *drawing* on that place?

My mind flashed back to the eruption of power we'd seen in the night sky after Wren was taken. A force so strong, it stripped our abilities from us like child's play.

I held my breathing steady. Didn't allow my muscles to move an inch. But only one word came to mind—one of Ulysses' favorites.

Fuck.

"Welcome." The voice reverberated around me as mist rose from the vat of blood. The fog did not dissipate, but instead coalesced to hang like a dense cloud above the red liquid that remained utterly still.

I resisted the urge to pull back. My gut shouted there was something watching me from within that fog—something to be avoided at all cost—even as my eye swore there wasn't anything there at all.

The rabids thought this thing was their god and king. I felt as if I was facing Hell's own Wizard of Oz.

"Gideon, son of Godwin," the voice continued. "That's the name you're known by, is it not? And Sentinel. How things change and yet stay the same."

"What do you want?" I demanded.

"To make the world the way it should have been."

My brow twitched down. At least now I understood where Amalie had gotten that turn of phrase. But what exactly it actually *meant*...

Primordial instincts argued I should fight or flee, but neither of those would serve me well at the moment—or be remotely possible. To flee would be to turn my back on this being, and I knew to my core that would be a mistake.

And how did you fight fog?

I let out a breath. Information gathering it was, then. Gods knew I needed that, anyway.

"How, precisely?" I asked, holding my voice calm and detached despite the fact I was conversing with a homicidal cloud. "Because at the moment, it appears you mean 'by killing the innocent.'"

The creature's voice turned rueful, as if grieved I didn't understand. "I'm saving them from themselves."

Incredulity made me scoff.

"Humans fight each other," the thing continued. "Kill each other. They have been doing this for countless millennia and without help, they'll do it for countless more. My own lands were torn apart by war after war and my people were barely surviving before I found the answer to our suffering. The pain I saw... such horrors..."

The pressure on my mind increased, images flashing at the edge of my awareness—starving children, people screaming from wounds so horrible it would have been a mercy to die.

"And all this simply because humans love to fight. It's in their blood"—a mild chuckle followed the words, as if Urlfeige enjoyed the pun—"at least, when they're left to their own devices. But when we bite them, when we put them in their proper place in the food chain, they are docile. They don't fight. They live peacefully."

My jaw tightened in spite of myself. "As blood slaves, stripped of their will."

"Stripped only of their baser nature. Is that truly so terrible?"

I couldn't find it in myself to respond. This was a fallacious argument to its core, and I suspected this creature knew that.

It just didn't care. Not if it believed it could convince me, regardless.

"Amalie tells me you love to read, to learn. Do you not do this to be a better person than the moment before? Constantly seeking growth. Yet you would deny this to them, when this flaw that causes them suffering is such a simple thing to correct?"

"That's not what you imply, nor what you're doing even now."

The amusement returned. "Isn't it?"

"You're butchering people. How many died for the jacuzzi of blood I see here?"

"Only the willing."

"*After* your people bit them, I'm sure. So no, not willing. Drugged. Even the humans you scorn know that does not equal consent."

"Consent." The creature scoffed. "Would you rather they consent to war? That is what you're offering them, for if they are left with the choice, they never stop waging it. All these millennia later, and they persist in slaughtering their own kind. In murdering children, and over what? So that they can own a scrap of land for a few decades before it's taken by another?" Urlfeige chuckled. "My enemies claimed I waged a war more horrible than most of their kind had ever seen. That the human species grew to fear the night, not because of tigers or wolves, but because of me. Yet, was that *truly* what happened? Yes, I had to kill some. Yes, a few survivors protested—*at first*. But once they understood, once they felt the lifesaving bite of my kind—*our* kind—they begged for what I offered."

Disgust made my insides roil. I could only imagine how those poor souls pled to be bitten again, reduced to little more than addicts craving another hit. Nothing would have mattered to them anymore. Not family, not friends. They'd sell their soul for us to sink our fangs into them one more time, and all their days would be but a waking dream, waiting for the moment when we'd feed from them again.

And we could reverse that, of course. The gods knew that if we or a dormant were ever so starved that we could not stop ourselves from feeding on a human, we fought every minute to keep that effect from taking hold, and we instantly released them from any trace of it the moment we were done.

Not so with rabids—though they rarely left anyone alive.

"*Lifesaving*," I repeated, unable to keep the contempt from my voice.

"Isn't it? Yes, we drink them. That's their place in the natural order. And in exchange, they are free of war, free of fear. They can walk through their streets without dreading that a killer might lurk in the shadows. They can raise their children in peace, never doubting for a moment their young will be safe. Compared to what they have wrought, this is a paradise. And you would deny them that?"

I stared at the fog and the gallons of blood beneath it. At the rabids standing by, severed body parts still in their grasp while they waited to begin feeding them to this thing again. Screams still echoed in the distance from the sealed rooms we'd passed on the way here. And all the while, Amalie smiled that same bloodthirsty grin I'd seen on her face whenever she returned from butchering whole villages and cities.

"You're mad," I said.

Urlfeige's voice dripped with amusement. "In the

kingdom of the mad, the sane man is always the one accused of such a thing."

The pressure in the air increased, the sheer weight of his presence bearing down on me.

"Serve me," Urlfeige said. "Let me into your mind, and I will show you the path to understanding and peace."

I gritted my teeth. "No."

Amalie made a baffled noise. "Why are you fighting this, Gideon?"

I couldn't respond. My head was pounding too hard.

"Is it her?" Amalie continued. "Resistance cost that stupid bitch everything. She can't keep this stubbornness going forever."

I twitched my eye over to her, confused. Who was she talking about? Wren?

"Where is she?" Urlfeige asked.

The pressure increased, and I grunted. My legs gave out under the weight of it, sending me to my knees.

"I could strip everything from you," Urlfeige said. "Your ability to extend your fangs, leaving you to starve. Your ability to survive on blood at all. Everything that makes you a vampire is mine to take."

The intensity of his presence grew, making my skull feel as if it would crack. My teeth ached like my fangs were being ripped from me, and my insides writhed like I was drying up and dying.

And yet, even now, the force of it was outside of my thoughts, unable to overwhelm my mind. I knew it wanted to. I could feel it clawing and scraping at the walls, seeking a weak point.

Finding none.

"Go to hell," I snarled.

A shout ripped from me as the pressure increased again, and concrete hit my shoulder as I collapsed to the floor. I could barely see the ground in front of me, my world reduced to the force of this being trying to shove its way into my mind.

Was this what he did to the dormants? To Ulysses?

My vision went dark. Pain ricocheted through me like a wild beast trying to escape.

"I will find her," Urlfeige said. "I will drain every thought from her mind, every ounce of blood in her body. One obstinate girl will never stand between me and the liberation of this world. If you wish to survive to enjoy it... surrender."

I couldn't speak, but it didn't matter. If this was where I ended, then I'd end knowing I never betrayed my fellow Sentinels.

Or Wren.

My heart ached. Being cut off from the Sentinels was a mercy, because then maybe they'd survive my death. They could go on, destroy this creature, and still protect her as well. And as for Wren, perhaps someday she'd forgive me for how I treated her.

But perhaps forgiveness was for others—and far too much to ask. Having honor now was all that remained. Even if I'd never gotten the chance to know her well, I'd seen how highly the others thought of her. I would never put her in harm's way.

Maybe that would have to be enough.

The pressure relented. Gasping, I blinked, my vision

coming back into focus. My heart still beat. Air still rushed to and from my lungs.

And the weight of Urlfeige's presence was withdrawing.

"Take him back to the cell," he said. "I will give him time to understand—as a courtesy."

The rabids hauled me from the ground, and my head swirled from the motion. The massive room blurred before my eyes when they spun me around, dragging me back toward the door again.

"The girl *will* be brought to heel, boy," Urlfeige called from behind me. "Your silence changes nothing. The day will come when you once again watch her scream as she dies."

I twisted, looking back at the creature, but the door slammed before I could form words.

Once again?

11

WREN

Three weeks later

*S*orry, *slower?* I signed.

I stared at Liam's hands in the firelight and then mimicked his motions.

Is that right? I asked.

He smiled, nodding.

I shifted my cross-legged position on the rug covering the hardwood floor and then repeated the sign four more times, trying to burn it into my memory. Ever since we'd come to this dilapidated old farmhouse courtesy of the mysterious Lazarus, who'd apparently won it in a card game from a bear shifter and then never looked at it again, I'd made it my mission to learn as much sign language as I could.

It wasn't like there were too many other demands on my time.

Letting out a breath, I repeated the other signs I'd been learning tonight. Beyond the cracked window, the sky was an indigo swath of darkness blanketing the empty fields surrounding the isolated farmhouse. We slept in shifts during the day now—like *real* vampires, I joked sometimes, not that I found it super funny—and stayed awake at night.

With rabids hunting for us, it seemed safer that way.

Now what? I asked when I finished.

At a fraction of the speed I knew he was capable of, Liam fingerspelled the next word and then showed me how to sign it. Nodding, I repeated it as well.

My family was safe, that much I knew. They'd called a few times, first from somewhere out in Wyoming if the area code was to be believed, and later from somewhere in California. Considering I'd never been to either state, it helped me breathe a little easier at the idea that maybe Amalie wouldn't find them. Meanwhile, Harper said Ollie and Emma had made it to Gateway City, wherever the hell that was. They even confirmed they'd heard from our friend Brayden in St. Louis, and he was fine too.

Irritated that school and the entire town of Fort Briar was now shut down, not to mention that all his friends had either vanished or wouldn't say where they were... but, you know, fine.

The GSS apparently had descended on Fort Briar only a short while after we all made it out, and now the town was off-limits to anyone. Chemical spill, they claimed.

Unsafe for anybody to come in. Survivors were being screened before they were sent packing—for potential toxic exposure, the slayers said, which would have been darkly ironic if not for the painful truth that they were probably killing anyone who'd been turned.

And so college was over for the semester, and my friends had wisely decided not to tell Brayden why. They couldn't. Not without infinitely harder conversations about being vampires and shifters and half-angels. Brayden was loyal as hell and would never leave us to face it alone, no matter how insane it all would surely sound. He'd come to help anyway.

He'd get killed.

So they'd left him in the dark, and I was guiltily grateful for it. Yes, there was footage of what happened in Fort Briar. Videos had spread online even while the rabids were attacking. But the GSS apparently had a technical wing, and nearly instantaneously, they'd marshaled an army of bots to discredit every single recording as being fake or, at best, a stupid social media challenge gone wrong. They'd generated images of the chemical spill too, all to counteract the "vampire hoax."

No one in the great wide world would believe it was vampires, not if the GSS had anything to say about it.

I wasn't upset about that part, either. Not really. The world finding out vampires were real probably would have been rough on a good day, too. Having them discover it because an entire town's worth of them had gone rabid and killed everyone they could get their hands on?

It'd be chaos. Mass hysteria.

War.

So we hid here and let the GSS sweep everything under the rug, all while hoping no rabids—or dormants—found us. Over the past few weeks, everything had settled into a bizarre sort of rhythm. Liam taught me sign language. Asher taught me to fight and use the sword—even if most of the time it felt more like I was remembering than learning, as if, left to its own devices, my body would already know what to do.

Which was weird as hell.

During the day, I slept in Asher's arms while Liam kept watch, at least until it was time for them to trade off. Early on, Asher snuck into a nearby town and found us some bagged blood to drink. It tasted like generic powdered juice mix compared to the rich wine that feeding from Asher or Ulysses had been, but at least this way, we wouldn't drain each other too badly or have to survive off of snack cubes alone.

Everything was strategy now. How to keep our strength up. Escape routes if vampires found us. Off and on, we'd argued about what to do. I wanted to find Eden and see if she could fix this, while Asher and Liam seemed hell-bent on making sure no one—not Amalie, not Urlfeige, not God himself—could possibly lay a hand on me. For weeks we hadn't been able to agree on that account, and so we stayed put while life fell into a holding pattern and we waited to see what Amalie and the monster behind her, Urlfeige, would do next.

And waited to see if anyone spotted Ulysses or Gideon, wherever the hell they were.

Liam tapped the floor in front of me, and I looked up.

Where'd you go? he asked, a gentle expression on his face.

I winced. "Sor—" I cut off, switching to sign language. *Sorry.*

His eyebrow rose.

I sighed. *Just thinking.*

You want to stop?

I shook my head, but he still paused before nodding in return.

It's going to be okay. He gave me an encouraging look.

I nodded, trying to believe that. I'd barely gotten the chance to know Ulysses or Gideon, but my heart was aching at the distance from them all the same. I couldn't imagine it was any easier for Liam or Asher either.

"Hey," he said, his voice rough. I glanced up again. *Have I told you about the time Asher accidentally became captain of a pirate ship?*

I choked on a laugh. *No. How?*

He grinned. *We'd set sail from South Carolina, but on our second day at sea, there was a storm.*

Tension leaked out of me as his story continued, a mix of signs I knew and fingerspelled words I didn't. It'd been like this for weeks now, Liam or Asher pulling me back from letting my thoughts spiral too much. Keeping my spirits up. Sharing their pasts in a way that somehow made me feel like everything was going to be all right. I couldn't describe how much I appreciated what they were doing.

But I loved them for it.

I hadn't said that to either of them, of course. It felt too weird in the midst of everything we were going through, telling them that, more than just being overwhelmingly attracted to them, I'd found myself falling for them too. Falling for their intelligence and humor and kindness. For the way Asher's eyes lit up when he laughed, and how Liam's lips had this funny little quirk when he smiled. For the empathy that seemed to come so naturally to Liam, and how, without me even saying a word, he could see when I was hurting. And how Asher looked at me with this quiet confidence like he believed I could do anything, even when I'd just landed on my ass while training.

I couldn't tell them that.

It was still true.

But the pirate captain didn't trust his first mate, Liam continued. *And since the captain had been wounded in the storm, this was a problem.*

A smile spread over my face as he told me of the bargain Asher struck with the captain to protect the survivors, of the way Gideon had bonded with crew from a dozen different backgrounds, and how Ulysses had regaled them all with stories of adventures that might have been only partly fiction, not that the crew would know that.

What about you? I asked when he finished.

He shrugged dismissively. *Not much to tell. I killed the rabids who had gotten on board, and no one questioned us again.*

My brow twitched down. I'd seen Liam in action, even just a little bit. It couldn't have been that simple. Had the crew been afraid of him? Pale as death, voice gone, fighting ability like a force of nature itself. Was that when the stories of the Sentinel who was basically the Grim Reaper began to spread?

Hey. He bent slightly to catch my eye. *What's wrong?*

I hesitated. *Were they scared of you?*

He paused and then bowed his head briefly. *Yes.*

There was no apology or self-pity on his face. The truth simply was.

I know what people say about me, he continued. *That I'm Death incarnate. That I'm insane.* His shoulders shrugged. *I don't know. Maybe I am.* His pale-blue eyes watched me in the firelight. *Does that scare you?*

I shook my head.

Mild surprise tinged his expression. *Why not?*

Only one answer came to me. *Because I don't think you are. You're protective. You would kill anything that threatened me. I know that. But you would never hurt me.*

He said nothing for a moment, the surprise on his face turning to something else. Gratitude, maybe, but sincerity and gentleness too. He reached over, his fingertips coming to rest on my knee, and my breath caught.

"Never," he whispered like a promise.

My lip slipped from between my teeth. Cautiously, I inched my hand toward his, ready to pull away in a heartbeat if he looked uncomfortable. But over the past few weeks, he'd been touching me more. A hand to my back here, a brush of my arm there, lingering longer each time. It almost felt like he was working up to something, and I knew what I *hoped* it might be.

I traced my fingertip along the side of his hand. "Is this okay?"

He nodded. His hand turned, wrapping gently around my fingers, pulling me closer to him.

My heart was pounding. I wetted my lips, and his blue eyes flicked down briefly, watching the motion.

"May I kiss you?" he asked softly.

I gave a tiny nod, a thrill running through me. "Please."

The corner of his mouth rose. Carefully, he moved closer, watching my face like he was waiting for the slightest hint I wanted him to pull away. He smelled like crisp winter air, like woodsmoke and pine and something just *him*, and it was intoxicating.

He kissed me lightly, a ghost of his lips across mine, and then he paused. His eyes closed for a moment. I didn't dare move.

And then he returned, harder, more determined. My lips parted for him, and a heartbeat later he was deepening the kiss, exploring me like I was his first taste of water after ages in the desert. With effort, I kept my hands on the floor at my sides, no matter how much I wanted to pull him to me, on top of me, to devour him with the same intensity that he was kissing me.

But far too soon, he was drawing back again.

My breaths came short and fast. This might be it, I knew. I had to accept that. My body was already aching for him, but I wouldn't push.

His eyes searched mine, and a touch breathlessly, he asked. "May we... do more?" His head tilted toward the pile of sleeping bags beneath the window that had formed the bed for the past few weeks.

A smile spread over my face immediately. "Yeah."

The corner of his mouth rose again, and his hand slipped down to mine. Rising to his feet, he brought me with him across the room. At the side of the sleeping bags, he paused.

My lips parted, but he didn't try to kiss me. His hand left mine only to tease along the hem of my shirt.

I didn't move. This was going to go at his pace or not at all. About that, I was determined.

Slowly, he drew my shirt up. I lifted my arms, letting him take it off me entirely.

The fabric fell to the ground without either of us giving it a glance. As my arms lowered back to my sides, his gaze roamed over me, taking in my breasts beneath my blue satin bra like he'd never seen anything like me in his life.

Gingerly, I reached out. "May I?" I whispered, not touching the edge of his shirt.

He gave a small nod.

I took the fabric, drawing it up carefully. He might feel trapped when it went over his head, I knew. This might be as far as we got... at least tonight.

Hope fluttered like a trapped bird in my chest. We'd crossed a threshold tonight, and even if this ended, maybe more could be to come. The moment he wanted to stop, I would. But, God, my body was throbbing for him.

The shirt passed over his head, and I dropped it to the floor. His chest rose and fell a bit quickly, but he made no move to retreat.

I stared at him. He was breathtaking. Lean but made of pure muscle, every line of him carved like it came from marble, leaving nothing to spare. Pale scars crisscrossed his skin, and on some level, I'd expected them. I knew what Amalie had done to him, all those centuries ago. I knew how she'd made sure the scars would stay no matter how vampires could heal—a sadist wanting to be reminded of her handiwork. But that wasn't what I saw. All of it only showed how he was stronger than her, every single line a testimony to the fact she'd failed to break him.

I lifted my eyes to his. He was watching me too, as if waiting to see how I reacted.

"Do you want to stop?" he asked quietly.

My head shook immediately. "Do you?"

"No."

He stepped closer, and I swallowed hard. I ached for him, so wet already.

Gently, he took my chin, tilting my face up toward his. He bent, kissing me again, softly at first, but soon his other hand was on my back, holding me closer. My breasts brushed his chest, and my nipples tingled with the desire to escape the satiny fabric and feel more of him.

His lips left mine, but before disappointment could gain a hold, he was kissing down the side of my throat.

Exhilaration coursed through me as I leaned my head to the side. If he bit me...

God, I wanted him to bite me.

"Yes," I whispered. "Please."

His hand tightened against my back, but when he reached the curve between my neck and my shoulder, he paused. I could feel his breathing, short and slightly fast. God, had I pushed him too far?

"Soon?" he whispered, not moving away.

I nodded quickly. "Yeah."

He was still for a moment longer, and then his hand climbed to the clasp on my bra. "May I?"

Again, I nodded. "Yes."

The bra loosened and dropped to the floor between us. His hands moved down to my jeans, tracing along the hem.

"Please?" I asked.

He unfastened them, drawing the denim down to my ankles and staying on his knees as I stepped out of the jeans. My panties were still in place, soaking from my desire for him, and I could barely breathe at how he was only inches from my pussy.

"I need you, Liam," I whispered.

His eyes flicked up to mine, hot and filled with desire, and the words seemed to galvanize him. He rose, his hand taking my own, and he nodded for me to lie down on the sleeping bags.

I sank onto the cushioning fabric, my whole body turned on to have him standing there looking down at me. His eyes roamed over me as my nipples ached for his touch and my clit throbbed with need.

Lowering himself down, he reached out again, playing his fingers along the edge of my panties, and it was all I could do not to beg. But when I gasped softly, his eyes returned to mine, and a thrill shot through me at the dark and wicked light in his gaze now.

Oh, God, he knew exactly what he was doing to me. Even if touch was difficult for him, even if every moment of this felt precarious, he still knew.

And he was enjoying it.

With torturous slowness, he pulled my panties away, exposing my soaking pussy to the air. His fingers ghosted along my thighs and around the sides of my knees as he drew the delicate cloth down, the light touch making me throb. As he pulled them away entirely and eased my legs apart, I whimpered, desperate for him to fill me right now.

He paused, and frantic need pulsed through me. "Please," I begged. "Please don't stop. I—"

Bending closer, he teased a finger along my slit, and I gasped, words abandoning me. Lifting it to his lips, he tasted me on his fingertip, his eyes never leaving mine.

I literally gulped.

He smiled and moved between my legs. Watching my face as he bent down, he traced his tongue along the same path his finger had taken. A breathless begging sound left me, and he didn't keep me waiting, diving in deeper to circle my clit, making me moan. His fingers returned, slipping into my entrance, stroking me from the inside.

"Yes," I breathed. "Oh, Liam, yes."

His pace increased. He needed to know this was okay with me, I realized. At every step, he needed to know I wanted it as much as he did.

My words turned to inarticulate pleading, and my hands fisted the sleeping bag as my whole body tightened from what he was doing to me. I wouldn't let myself touch him, not until I knew he was okay with it. But God...

The orgasm hit me like a tidal wave, and I threw my head back, crying out his name as pleasure surged through me, obliterating the world. I was in heaven, and he didn't stop wringing the pleasure from me for a second as it pulsed through my veins.

God, he knew *exactly* what he was doing.

At long last, my body sagged back to the sleeping bags, and I looked at him, panting from my release. A smile pulled at my lips, and I was pretty sure the fabric beneath us was soaked from both him and me. But as he grinned back, wiping his face clean, I could still see his cock straining against his pants.

Desire bubbled up in me, my body concluding in an instant that I wasn't actually done.

My eyes rose back to his, slowly and deliberately, as I let my legs fall apart again. "More?"

A hint of trepidation flashed over his face. I bit my lip, worried that maybe I'd asked for too much, too soon. It was his call on how far he felt comfortable taking this, but whatever he wanted, I was *so* here for it.

The trepidation faded like he'd shut it away somewhere, and only desire remained. Rising to his feet, he unfastened his pants and pushed them and his underwear down.

My body was *definitely* not done. Hunger for him to be in me throbbed through my core at the sight of him. His body may have been lean, but his cock made my insides clench in anticipation of feeling that thick shaft thrusting into me. God, I needed him to have me, claim me, take me right the fuck now, because in this moment I was utterly certain that, as much as I was the others', I was his too.

And he was mine.

He lowered himself down and moved over me, his arms bracing him above my body. His blue eyes searched mine, his whole body tense.

My legs spread farther for him. "Is this okay?" I whispered.

His head dipped in a single nod. "Yes."

Desire propelled my words. "Then take me, Liam. Make me yours too."

He smiled.

12

———————

LIAM

If my heart beat any harder, it would break free of my chest. Somewhere inside, the old bastard of anxiety still clamored, but I'd spent these past few weeks at the farmhouse working ceaselessly to train my body and mind that—when it came to Wren—I was safe.

And now the most beautiful woman I'd ever seen was begging me to enter her, and I'd be damned if I denied her.

I lowered myself over her body. Her taste still clung to me, and her heady scent filled my head, making my cock ache with need for her. As my tip reached her entrance, it was all I could do not to groan, while on either side, her fists gripped the sleeping bag again.

It wasn't from fear. Every sound she made, every plea, let me know that. If I had to guess, I thought she was keeping herself from touching me, as if determined not to risk pushing me too far.

I loved her for that. I wanted her hands all over me,

but not yet. Not now. Now, I wanted to give her this and not lose myself to old anxieties, because the truth was, I needed her too.

She was mine. Ours. Every molecule of my being knew it, and there could be no question. Wren belonged to the Sentinels.

And we belonged to her.

"Please, Liam," she whispered.

I rocked my hips forward, sliding my cock into her tight wetness and warmth, and I couldn't stop myself from groaning this time. Her soaked pussy gripped me, working me as I bottomed out balls-deep inside her and then pulled out and thrust into her again.

A smile spread over her face, giving me strength to shove any lingering anxieties to the back of my mind. She wanted this. Begged for it, even, and by all that was holy, I'd never deny her.

And someday, I'd drink from her.

The thought made anxiety try to rise again, but I succeeded in crushing it down and letting it be overwhelmed by desire. I wanted to drink from her. With my whole heart and soul, I did. But feeding... It felt as intimate as this, and right now, I wanted to give to her, not take.

She moaned beneath me, and instinctively, my pace picked up. Harder and harder, I thrust into her as pleasure made her head lie back and her eyes close. A flush touched her cheeks with pink, and her full lips parted as she gasped.

"Yes," she breathed. "Oh, God, yes."

My own orgasm pushed at me, threatening to bring

this to an end, and I fought it back. I wouldn't come until she did, dammit. She was mine and I was hers and watching her release was one of the most beautiful things I'd ever seen.

Her pleading words became ragged, and her breathing did too. Beneath me, her body rocked, every motion punctuated by a whimper of need that grew more frantic with every moment.

Pride filled me. I could give her this. I really could bring our incredible woman pleasure, and that fact overwhelmed any fear, any doubt.

A cry left her as her hands clenched down on the blankets and her pussy spasmed around me, pulsing as the orgasm took her.

And I couldn't hold back any longer.

With a savage roar of pure ecstasy, I came inside her, driving myself into her until I had nothing left and my muscles threatened to give way. My heart raced and I gasped for air as I slid from within her and rolled to the side, lying on the sleeping bags as the world returned.

Old anxiety lapped at the edges of the orgasmic afterglow, and I closed my eyes, trying to drive it away. I had no illusions that this fixed everything or that I'd never struggle again, but this had also been more than I'd ever thought I would have with someone.

I couldn't wait to do it again.

At my side, Wren rolled over to face me.

The anxiety grew stronger, more for what she might say now than anything. Bracing myself, I shifted around to face her as well.

"Thank you," she said softly.

And just like that, the old bastard receded. "Thank you too," I replied.

She smiled. "Any time you want to do that again..."

Satisfaction spread through me in a warm glow. I could bring her pleasure, and feel it too, and if I never touched another being in all my centuries, I didn't care.

Not when I had her.

I leaned closer, taking her cheek, drawing her to me and kissing her with all the love I couldn't begin to find the words to say.

13

ASHER

The morning sun peeked over the horizon, tingeing the misty fields with pink and pale gold, and birds chirped in the trees, enjoying the dawn.

Sheer willpower kept me watching it, when all I wanted to do was leave my chair on the porch and head back into the house. Even if I hadn't possessed the connection binding me to the other Sentinels, I could have heard what was happening in there, despite how part of me couldn't quite believe it.

Liam... with Wren. What it must have taken for him to push past the pain that kept him from allowing anyone close left me dumbstruck—and happy as hell for him. I wouldn't disrupt the two of them for anything, no matter how much my cock was pleading for me to go in the house already and join him in pleasuring her. I wanted her so badly it hurt. But I wanted them to have this together too.

I shifted my aching cock in my pants as another wave of desire and need and pleasure beat at my brain. Surprisingly, I was fairly sure it wasn't just Liam I was picking up on. I could feel a connection to Wren as well. It was different than my link to the others, though gods help me if I could explain how. My connection to them had defined my life for so long, I could barely remember a time when it hadn't been there. But slowly over these past few weeks, it felt like the shape of it was shifting. No longer a web between us all.

Now it was more like spokes on a wheel.

And she was at the center.

I rubbed my palms along my thighs, focusing as hard as I could on the empty fields around the old farmhouse and *not* what was happening upstairs. Lazarus hadn't been kidding when he told me the place wasn't much to look at. An aging two-story house with a wraparound porch that had collapsed on one side, and a fallen oak tree in the yard that had apparently missed hitting the house by inches. The three of us had taken to staying in the only upstairs bedroom that still had glass in the windows— Wren sleeping curled up against me, Liam keeping watch, though now I wondered if he'd like to trade off on that instead. I loved holding her, but I didn't mind if he wanted to do the same.

There was something so comforting, knowing she felt safe enough to rest in our arms.

I gritted my teeth, forcing my thoughts away from the feel of her or the residual waves of pleasure coming from upstairs. Tracking the slight movements of animals in the brush around us could be important. Or watching the gravel road fifty yards away, separated from this property by a ramshackle wooden fence with probably a quarter of its beams missing. Sure, the only things I'd seen all morning were the deer picking their way through the mist rolling across the fields on the other side of the road. The animals never strayed too far from the trees on the far end of the field, though, preferring to stay close to the safety of the shadows and the river hidden there. And the mist itself didn't have the feel of rabids at all. Meanwhile, there wasn't another neighbor for at least five miles in any direction, and I hadn't seen or heard a car the entire time we'd been here.

Gods below, I wanted to get my ass up there and see how many more orgasms the two of us could give Wren.

My phone buzzed in my pocket, and I grabbed at it in desperation for anything else to focus on.

Wariness prickled through me at the sight of the number.

Lazarus.

I clicked through to the text message. A video link waited inside, and I checked quickly that the audio on my phone was at a decent level before tapping on it.

Cold horror pressed down on me as the images played across my screen.

"Oh, hell," I whispered.

14

WREN

The early morning light spread over the ceiling, chasing away the shadows. At my side, Liam rested on the sleeping bags.

And I was in heaven.

Sex with Liam had been better than I ever could have imagined. My body still felt like it was thrumming from the orgasms he'd given me. And as for the idea that he wanted to do it again? And that maybe, just *maybe* Asher could be convinced to come up and join us too?

Yeah. Heaven.

I smiled. God, a few months ago, I never could have imagined this would be my life. I wouldn't have wanted the bad parts, of course, and I was definitely worried for my family, the other Sentinels, and—let's be honest—the world. But to be lying here with this gorgeous man? To be hoping another incredible man would join us later for more?

Um, no. Not something I'd ever have dreamed would happen to me.

And now I didn't want to imagine my life without them.

Beside me, Liam stirred, and I looked over to find him watching me, a hint of a smile playing at his lips. I grinned, blushing, though I couldn't say why. It was a bit late to be modest. But the look in his eyes made me feel like I was the only person in the universe.

His hand rose, making a small gesture. *Beautiful.*

My blush deepened. His fingers came up to my cheek, and I didn't miss the small hitch in his breathing a millisecond before his skin brushed against mine. Every bit of this was incredible, but I wasn't so vain as to let myself believe that touching would suddenly become easy for him just because we'd shared this.

But anything he wanted to do, I was *so* ready for it.

Shifting around a bit, he drew closer and gently gave me another kiss. I flicked my tongue along his lips, inviting, hoping, and I felt him grin before he returned, taking me up on the offer.

A cold shiver of alarm shot through me like a needle of ice.

Liam was moving immediately, breaking away from my lips and leaving the bed with lightning speed. The early morning light played over the carved lines of his muscles as he checked through the window for any threats, every inch of his naked body radiating the tension of a predator on the verge of attacking.

I sat up, adrenaline making my heart race. I strained to hear anything from outside, but there was nothing. The cold chill of *something is wrong* pebbled my bare skin, but I couldn't tell why. There was no breeze in the room to make me cold, and beyond the window, birds chirped happily away while the rising sun touched the trees with purple and pink.

Barely taking his eyes from the window, Liam pointed to my clothes on the floor. The gesture was more than clear. Scrambling up, I pulled on my clothing as fast as I could while he retrieved his own from the ground nearby, his eyes still flashing between the window and the door as if waiting to see where the threat would come from first.

My hands shook as I tugged my jeans into place. I still couldn't hear anything from outside, and surely if Asher was in trouble, that wouldn't be the case.

Unless someone actually managed to sneak up on him...

Panic drummed a fast beat in my chest. This weird feeling wasn't *pain*, exactly. Alarm and horror, maybe, and it hurt, but it wasn't mortal agony.

Like I could know that for sure. I didn't even know what this *was*, but if anyone had hurt Asher...

My hand moved before I even registered the impulse, and suddenly the sword was in my hand, dancing with cold, white fire. Liam's eyes flashed over to it, and instantly, his knife was in his fist.

A knock came on the door.

I froze. Rabids wouldn't knock.

The door opened slowly, and Asher peered inside. At the sight of us, he paused, but the grave look on his face didn't change.

Oh, God... my family. Or Ulysses and Gideon, or any of my friends. Something horrible had happened.

"What's wrong?" I asked, bracing myself all over again. My fist clenched around the hilt of the sword, even if there wasn't any need for it. But the blade felt comforting and familiar, as if my body recognized it on some deep level even if I didn't know why. But suddenly, I wanted that.

The weapon *was* me, somehow, and I was damn well ready to use it.

Asher hesitated. "Ulysses."

My mouth moved. He was dead. He was hurt. He was—

I yanked my thoughts off the rails of panic. "What about him?"

"Someone spotted him in St. Louis." He paused. "It's not good."

Horror gripped me. Brayden. My best friend had been in Saint—

I shoved the thought down. "Not good how?"

Asher pulled out his cell, and then he hesitated, grim reluctance crossing his face. He made no move to turn the screen on.

"*Show me*," I insisted.

His mouth tightened, but he unlocked the phone and tapped an icon. Warily, I came closer as he held up the screen, Liam right behind me.

For a moment, the video was so dark, I couldn't make out any details. Scratching noises like shoes on gravel were the only sound, but then the image changed. For a moment it was unclear, as if the person was crouched behind something, hiding, but then the camera focused on a stretch of concrete and gravel at the heart of a collection of warehouses.

But it wasn't empty. A dozen figures dressed in black leather like the rabids who attacked us stood in a loose circle around six people huddled on the ground. The camera shook for a moment as if the person holding it had shifted position, and then the image zoomed in.

It wasn't just a dozen rabids.

Ulysses faced the cowering people, nothing but ice on his face. It wasn't the hateful look he'd given me all those weeks ago, back when he thought I was Amalie in disguise. It wasn't rage. There was just *nothing* in his eyes, like the crying people ahead of him weren't even insects.

My eyes darted over the faces of every human I could see, searching for anyone familiar.

"Please," a man begged, his voice thin over the distance from the person recording this. The guy's gaze whipped around, trying to keep the circling rabids in sight. "Whatever you want. Just let us go. We're not your enemy, and we won't—"

Ulysses lunged at him, and blood erupted everywhere as he tore into the man.

I spun away, my gorge rising as screams came from the phone behind me, cut off quickly as Asher ended the video. But that couldn't erase the horrors I'd seen.

But Brayden hadn't been there, and I hated that some part of me was relieved by that.

"What... the *hell*?" I whispered.

Asher looked sickened as he tucked his phone away. "I don't know."

"Amalie," Liam said, rage thickening his rough voice.

"Or Urlfeige. Whatever they did..." Asher's head shook. "That's not Ulysses. He would *never*..."

I gulped down a breath. "So what do we do?"

From the corner of my eye, I saw Liam sign something too fast for me to catch. Asher turned away, grimacing.

"What?" Neither of them answered me. "Dammit, what?"

"We know what Ulysses would want us to do," Asher said.

I hesitated, lost, and then a chilling certainty rolled over me. "No. No, we're not killing him."

Asher didn't respond.

"No! We are figuring a way out of this for us *and* him, do you hear me? You told me that connection thing between you all meant if one of you died, the others would too, so you can't—"

Asher glanced back at me, and the look in his eyes made my heart thump oddly in my chest. It was like warmth but sorrow and iron, and I could just read it. He intended to stop this.

Whatever it took.

"We just need to *find* them," I insisted. "Get Ulysses and—I don't know—take him to Eden or a witch or *some-body* who can fix this, okay? That's it."

The iron in his expression strengthened. "*We* don't. I can track him, but I'm not bringing you anywhere near—"

"What? No!" Panic gripped me, and I took a step forward. "We've had this debate, Asher. He's already rabid. Whatever this is that happens to vampires who see me, it won't happen to him. So I still think we should go to Eden.

Maybe she can fix him and whatever is going on with me too."

"And if Amalie or Urlfeige find you on the way? We don't know how many people they've turned. How many rabids are out there anymore. And that doesn't even bring the GSS and Consortium into it." He stared at me like he couldn't fathom why I was arguing this. "You saw what he did. I will handle him on my own and—"

"You're not serious."

Frustration flashed over his face. "Dammit, we don't know what we're up against! Strategically, the smartest move is to risk as little as possible, and that means you stay here with Liam."

I gaped at them both, watching as Liam looked away with a grimace while Asher's determined expression didn't change at all. "*Strategically*?" I repeated. "What if she's gotten Gideon as well?" My stomach twisted at the thought, but I pressed onward. "Then it'll be two against one, and that's without counting all the rabids. And what happens if she does whatever this is to you too? Then it's me and Liam against all of you." I shook my head. "No, if we stick together, then you and Liam can watch each other's backs." I tightened my grip on the sword. "And so can I."

His eyes dropped to the glowing blade.

Self-consciousness suddenly tinged my rage, like I was a little kid caught playing with grown-up things, and I hated the feeling. Stuffing it down beneath indignation, I glared at him. "Look, I may not be as skilled as any of you, and yes, there's this weird thing that happens to the other vampires around me. But I'm damn well not useless."

His jaw muscles jumped. "I didn't say you were."

"Then we go together."

"No, I—"

"Dammit, I'm not hiding while you go out and get killed!"

"And I'm not watching you die!"

I stared at him, my chest rising and falling in rapid breaths. "Asher—"

"No." His head shook. "No, I won't—"

I crossed the room and took his hand, pouring every ounce of belief I could into my voice as I said, "We're going to make it. We *are*, okay? But if we split up, it'll leave us in more danger. You. Me and Liam. All of us. Because you're right, we don't know what we're up against, and yes, there are weird things going on, but facing them alone..." Certainty weighed down on me like there was no other answer in the universe. "We *have* to stick together."

Pain carved tense lines on his face, and when he spoke, his voice was thick. "I'm not losing you on top of everyone else who—"

I rose up on my toes, wrapping my free hand around his neck, and I kissed him. For a heartbeat, he froze, and then he was right there, devouring me. One hand raked up through my hair to keep me with him and his other gripped my back, crushing me to him while his tongue plundered me as if to convince himself I was here and alive.

I felt the sword vanish, and immediately I reached out. Liam gripped my hand. Pulling him closer, I broke from Asher's lips to look at them both. "We stay together," I said. "And we find Eden and see if she can stop this some-how. All of it. Okay?"

The two men's eyes met, something unspoken passing between them. An understanding, maybe.

"Okay," Asher said.

The solemnity in their expressions made determination coil in my gut and shivers run over my skin. I nodded to him, making my own quiet promise to myself that *nothing* would happen to them. Not Asher, not Liam, and damn well not Ulysses or Gideon either.

I wouldn't lose my Sentinels.

15

WREN

Arriving near Eden's cottage in an SUV, rather than via flying vampire, felt wildly different than the first time I'd visited the witch.

Of course, that time I'd been clinging to reality by my fingernails, all because four hot guys were determined to convince me I was a vampire.

Now I was clinging to the hope Eden could save them.

Asher pulled the SUV to a stop as the narrow road came to an end in a wall of trees and bushes, as if whoever made the gravel track had simply given up on going any farther into the forest. Leaning closer to the windshield, he scanned the woods and the sky briefly before pushing open the driver's side door and climbing out. On the passenger side, Liam looked back at me and nodded.

I got out. Past the treetops, the sky was turning that deeper tone of blue that it took on in the afternoon, like the sun had slowly baked the pale blue of morning into a more weathered and tired shade. White wisps of cloud drifted overhead, and a few birds flew past, unbothered by the fact three vampires were walking below.

I couldn't hear anything out here. No people, no traffic. Just sounds of nature and the rustle of my own footsteps while I followed Asher toward the trees. But as I trailed him along a winding path through the forest, I couldn't keep from checking around nervously. Sure, rabids wouldn't last long out here—unless they'd gone full leather-clad-apocalypse like the ones at Ollie and Emma's apartment—but that didn't mean Ulysses or Gideon might not be nearby. And given that Asher and Liam both said they hadn't been able to feel any connection to them since they were taken, we'd have no warning if they attacked.

By the time the trees parted and Eden's cottage came into view, I felt drawn tighter than a guitar string. The squat building showed no sign of trouble, though it'd be hard to know for sure if the ramshackle structure had ever suffered any damage. Nearly lost beneath its thick blanket of moss and ivy, the building looked a feather's weight away from collapsing completely. Unlike last time I was here, though, I didn't buy the image for a moment. In fact, now that I'd met the witch inside, I suspected it was a disguise of some kind, though I had no idea against what.

I glanced at the glistening glass ornaments and strange baubles hanging from tree limbs all around. The few closest to us stirred, twisting as if in a breeze though the wind was still, while the others were motionless.

A silent alarm system, maybe?

Carefully, Asher started forward into the clearing, taking each step as if expecting a trap to spring. With a wary glance at Liam, I followed while the other Sentinel moved in behind me, the three of us inching toward the winding path between the carefully tended gardens that fronted the run-down cottage.

The door opened before we made it more than a few feet. "Figured I'd be seeing you eventually," came a young woman's voice. "If you weren't dead, anyway."

Despite her wry tone, Eden's face was tense as she regarded us from her doorway. Dark circles showed beneath her eyes, and her face had a gaunt look, as if she hadn't eaten or slept in a while. Her long light-brown hair was lashed back in a messy ponytail, and she wore a hoodie with the faded logo of a local band above her paint-stained jeans.

Asher paused. "Are you okay?"

"Fine."

I didn't buy the swift response, and from the cautious way they were watching her, neither did Asher or Liam.

Eden made a dismissive noise. "Witch business. Plus, there's an ancient vampire warlord on the loose who's apparently feeding off the empty realms, so, you know, lots on my mind. Which brings me to the question…"

All around the yard, the baubles and ornaments on the trees began to spin, each rotating in sync with the others, while in the garden every plant suddenly turned its leaves our way. Even the house itself suddenly felt less like a run-down mess, and more like a beast that had only made us think it was sleeping and now waited for the command to strike. The air suddenly became hard to breathe, thick and heavy with power, as if energy was rising like floodwaters from the earth itself.

"What the hell are you doing here?" Eden finished. "Did that thing send you?"

I trembled. She hadn't even moved a *muscle* to make all this happen.

"No one sent us." Asher's voice was tense. "We've come for your help."

A ragged laugh left her, as if that was somehow ironic. But after a moment, the cold humor drained and caution took its place in her eyes. "There's something different about you. All of you, but..." Her eyes tracked over me. "You most of all."

"The rabids pulled Amalie out of my mind," I said. "One of them let Amalie take her over."

"Huh."

There was nothing in her tone. I could have just told her the price of asparagus in France for all the interest she showed.

But the ornaments started spinning faster.

"Amalie has Ulysses and Gideon," Asher said. "She's turned at least one of them into... something else. Maybe both."

Nothing in the clearing changed. The ornaments spun. The air felt like we were sinking into mud that would swallow us whole.

Shivers crawled over my skin, and it took effort to keep my hand from twitching with the urge to summon the sword. I honestly wasn't sure whether the blade would work against any of this—or even what to attack. But I couldn't let her hurt these men who mattered so much to me.

Her eyes flicked down to my motionless hand like she saw my struggle anyway.

"Please." I made my voice as placating as I could. "We need your help. You stopped Amalie from taking me over before. We need you to do something like that again."

She didn't look convinced. But she also didn't say anything.

"We're not here to be a threat to you, Eden," Asher said. "We swear."

A heartbeat passed. All around us, the ornaments slowly stopped spinning and the plants returned to their previous positions. Even the cottage felt like it was standing down while the thick energy on the air melted away.

Eden never took her eyes from me.

"Come inside." Without another word, she turned and disappeared into her house.

I'd never walked into the mouth of a dragon before, but that's pretty much what Eden's cottage felt like. Gone was the bubbling pot on the stove and the warm glow of candles. Now, the place held the twilight gloom of a cave. The pot wasn't in the empty fireplace, and in the loft above, the mattress stood bare, all its mismatched blankets gone, as if every bright or friendly thing had been stripped away. Even the lingering scents of pine and cinnamon and flowers felt ominous rather than comforting, like they might turn deadly if we made one wrong move.

I swallowed hard, looking for a source of the tension, but I couldn't find anything. Not that would hurt *her,* anyway. But on the mantel, I'd swear the pictures of people in pioneer clothing were watching us with sinister expressions, tracking our every step—even if, whenever I looked straight at them, they were smiling and not looking at me at all. Trinkets and crystals lay on the table nearby, nothing in me wanting to come within a dozen yards of them now, while the silver knife set among them glinted from more than the weak light through the windows.

"We're not here to hurt you," I said, though I felt like I was speaking to the house as much as to Eden. "Okay? We just need help."

I jumped as the door shut behind us without anyone touching it. On the other side of the room, Eden's lip twitched, her eyes tracking something away from the door before returning to us. "Talk," she ordered.

I floundered, not sure where to begin. "We saw Ulysses. Amalie's done something to him." I paused. "And any vampire who looks at me is turning rabid."

Her eyebrow twitched up ever so slightly at the last. Briefly, her attention flicked between Asher and Liam.

"Except them," I amended awkwardly.

"And what's different about you two versus the others?" Eden asked.

"We think it has something to do with our weapons," Asher said. "But we're not sure."

"Hmm."

I couldn't read anything from her tone, and without saying anything else, she turned away. Walking over to one of the side tables, her fingers strayed over the knick-knacks and crystals there, turning one, repositioning another without any apparent rhyme or reason.

I didn't take my eyes off her. I may not have known jack about magic, but something made me think that wasn't just nervous fidgeting on her part.

"You helped me with Amalie," I said carefully. "Gave me that pendant that kept her from taking over my mind. Could you do something similar now with this 'vampires go rabid at the sight of me' thing? And maybe give us something to break Ulysses and Gideon free too?"

Her eyes flicked back to me. "Think well of my abilities, don't you?" Her tone was wry again, but I'd swear something pained lurked under the surface.

"Eden, what's going on?" Asher asked, clearly concerned.

She was silent for a moment, and when she spoke, she ignored his question entirely. "The pendant I gave you worked because Amalie wasn't completely back in this world at the time. And that ancient vampire hadn't yet tried to fully exercise his power either. Neither of those things are still true, and whatever he's done..." She paused, thoughtful, her eyes on the baubles in front of her. "There is a piece missing."

I glanced from her to the trinkets and back, not sure if she meant the things on the table or something else entirely.

Somehow, I thought it was the latter.

Releasing a resolute breath, she turned back to us. "You know more than you're telling me." Her eyes flicked down to my hand.

The skin on my back prickled like the room itself was watching me. "I-I have a sword now. Like their knives."

"Why?"

My head gave a tiny shake. "I don't know. It just appeared."

Her eyes narrowed. "Nothing else happened?"

I started to say no, but memory played back. "A... a whisper? In my head? Not like Urlfeige—that vampire warlord you were talking about. Someone else."

"Who?"

My shoulders shrugged even as the answer spread through my body. *Me.*

"I'm not sure." I risked a glanced at Eden.

God, it felt like she was staring right through my skull and reading all the thoughts inside. I struggled not to fidget under the scrutiny. After a heartbeat, her gaze flicked to Asher and Liam, and then back to me again.

"I'd like to try something." She turned back to the trinkets, scanning them briefly and then glancing around the room as well.

"Try what?" I asked warily.

She drew up a crystal, turning it this way and that in the dim twilight like she was studying something in its depths. "To find the truth." Her brow cocked at me. "If you're willing."

"Will this hurt Wren?" Asher asked before I could speak.

"Only as much as the truth hurts."

Ice coiled in the pit of my stomach. I wasn't an idiot.

The truth could hurt like hell.

"Will this help Ulysses and Gideon?" I asked.

"Possibly."

I looked at Asher and Liam, seeing resistance on both their faces. But what was the alternative? Turning around, when this was our only option to do *anything* for those two? Short of racing in there, kamikaze style.

And probably getting killed.

I swallowed hard. "Okay, what do I need to do?"

"Wren..." Liam started.

"Ulysses needs our help. Gideon too. And I can't hide forever."

Eden motioned for me to take a chair beside one of the tables along the wall.

Keeping my steps steady and measured, I walked over to where she indicated. The house still felt like it was tracking my every move. When the wood chair creaked beneath me when I sat down, I half expected the thing to collapse under me from pure spite.

Eden's lip twitched like she could see my anxiety, and I didn't know what to make of the expression. The witch had seemed... well, intimidating, sure, when I first met her, but not malicious.

And maybe she still wasn't. Maybe the expression would have been kindly, if not for how the tension in the room was so thick, I could have cut it with a knife—and that was without bringing into it the sword that might appear in my hand.

I clenched my fingers together in my lap, hoping that would keep the sword away, if only to prevent the magical house from dropping the roof on my head. God, if ever there was a bad time for that weapon to show up...

Turning, Eden crossed to the kitchen and opened a

cupboard, taking down a trio of mismatched cups and tucking them in one arm. From the counter, she took a glass pitcher of water as well. Without explaining, she returned to us and set everything down on the table beside me.

"What's that for?" I asked.

She regarded the table for a moment before picking up one crystal after another, collecting them in her hand. "Take these." She gave several to me and then extended the rest to Asher and Liam, both of whom were watching her warily. "Go on."

The men took the crystals. Eden flashed a tight smile.

"Now—" She drew up the silver knife.

Protests came from Asher and Liam immediately, and I flinched back, my hands rising as if to defend myself.

"It's not meant to hurt her!" Eden snapped over their objections.

The two men fell quiet with cautious expressions. With an irritated sigh, Eden turned to me. "I need a drop of your blood. That's all."

"You swear on your goddess you mean her no harm?" Asher asked before I could respond.

Eden was silent for a moment. "As long as no one tries to harm me."

Asher and Liam paused for a heartbeat before their tension eased—albeit microscopically.

Seeming to take what she could get, Eden returned her attention to me. "A drop, please."

There wasn't much request in her tone. Trying not to show my nervousness—and probably failing miserably —I held out one of my hands, careful to keep my palm open just in case any ghostly swords decided to show up.

Quick as lightning, she pricked my finger, and I hissed between my teeth at the bite of the blade. Blood welled from the cut, and I'd swear I felt the tension rise in the Sentinels, even if neither of them moved a muscle. But nearly in unison, their eyes flicked down to the droplet, lingering there.

My body flushed at the desire in their eyes. None of us had taken any blood from one another in weeks out of fairness to Liam, who hadn't seemed at the time like he would join in on anything that followed—on top of not wanting to deplete each other if we needed our strength to fight. But bagged blood had nothing on drinking from one another. Heat spread through my core, just the thought making me wet, and my body trembled to imagine their hands on me, their fangs sinking into my skin, and their mouths moving on my flesh while their cocks thrust into me.

Both men tore their gazes away, fastening them on anything besides the blood on my hand, and awkwardness rose on the heels of my arousal. God, I didn't need to be thinking about this right now.

Seemingly ignoring us, Eden moved the knife delicately, drawing the droplet onto the blade, and then dipping it into the water pitcher. Reaching up to the hanging dried plants above her, she pinched off leaves with a practiced motion and deposited them in the pitcher as well. In steady rotations, she swirled the knife around, whispering.

My brow twitched down, a strange feeling moving

through me. I could barely hear her words, but they seemed to resonate in my mind, like something in me recognized them all the same.

Trepidation built in me, and Eden's gaze flicked over like she could sense my nervousness on the air, but she never stopped her motions or her silent whispering. With careful movements, she wiped the knife on a folded cloth nearby before setting it aside, and then she took up the pitcher, pouring the contents into the cups.

"Drink," she commanded, offering us one each.

I took it warily. The contents should have just looked like water with some herbs floating in it, but instead, the liquid was dark. I couldn't see the bottom of the cup.

Something inside me wanted to drink it, though. The feeling was irrational, like the weird impulse to jump when you were standing at the edge of a cliff. It didn't mean this was safe.

After all, if Eden wanted to poison us, this would probably be the best way.

My eyes rose to her and then slid to Asher and Liam. What choice did we have? Let me turn any vampire I laid eyes on into a rabid? Leave Ulysses and Gideon trapped with Amalie? *Abandon* them?

Nothing in me could do that. Simply nothing.

I lifted the cup, hesitating as it touched my lips. Eden wouldn't kill us.

Probably.

Bracing myself, I swallowed.

16

GIDEON

The latch clicked, and the door to the room that had become my cell swung open again.

I didn't bother looking up. For weeks, that mad rabid king had tried to overwhelm my mind.

And for weeks he'd failed.

I could only assume the fact I continued to possess my knife had something to do with it. We'd never truly known the source of those blades, though scholars had given us explanations over the years connecting back to angels and demons and all manner of things. But for the first time, I'd started to wonder if the weapons originated in the same empty realms from which Urlfeige drew his strength. Perhaps that was why they protected us.

But surely the knife would feel different if that were the case. More ominous. More *evil*.

The entire debate was merely a thought experiment, though. Only the torture was constant. Amalie played her games with knives, cutting me, leaving me covered in my own blood. I could only assume Urlfeige had as yet forbidden her from taking my eye—or perhaps she enjoyed knowing I could watch the torture—for even after all these weeks, I still could see. But in between her games and the stretches of silence where they forced blood down my throat to feed me and then left me hanging in chains, the king of the rabids tried day in and day out to shove his way into my mind.

The door swung shut again. "It'll be better when you give in, brother."

I gritted my teeth. He was back, then. This *thing* that was whatever Ulysses had become.

"You'll understand everything then. We are all better from this. Stronger."

"Brainwashed." I tossed the word out, glancing up at him. As with so many times before, he was splattered with blood. The gods only knew what he'd been doing.

How many he'd killed.

I had no illusions. This wasn't the friend and brother I'd known for centuries. But our skills made us deadly under the best conditions, and these were far from that.

Under the control of that madman, Ulysses would be a terrifying weapon.

"We're at peace," he countered. "Our minds are clear for the first time."

I grimaced, shaking my head. "I know you're in there somewhere, brother. I swear to you, I'll find a way to save you."

Ulysses chuckled and leaned back against the stone wall. "There's no one to save."

"Then explain how the man I've known for over eight

hundred years could stomach walking around with what is *probably* the blood of innocents on him?"

He glanced down and shrugged dismissively.

An incredulous noise escaped me. "The Ulysses I know would be tormented by such a thing. It would remind him of the night Amalie slaughtered his family. It always did."

He regarded me, not a trace of recognition or concern in his eyes, and my brow twitched down. If ever I'd wanted evidence he was *not* himself...

Cold suspicion prickling through me, I persisted, "Do you recall that? Your family? *Anyone*?"

"I know what it matters to know."

Oh, by the gods...

"Then tell me your memories," I demanded. "Show me you remember who you were. Because if you do not, there is no *way* I will believe you truly think this a better life. If that creature needed to take your identity from you just to craft you into his henchman, this wasn't a free choice you made at all."

He shook his head at me, picking idly at the blood crusted beneath his fingernails. "You're being a fool, brother."

"Better a fool who knows who he is than a puppet with no history."

He sighed as if despairing of me.

The sound galvanized me. If some shred of him persisted in there, perhaps this could wake it up. "Should I tell you your past, then, *brother*? Should I remind you of the family you loved so dearly? Your sister who wove fabric so beautiful you said it rivaled the flower fields we saw in Holland and Japan. Your father and the olive orchard that was his pride and joy. Do you remember the taste of those olives? The feel of that fabric in your hands?"

A bored expression on his face, he didn't even look my way.

Rage and desperation pushed at me. The gods help me, I knew how it hurt the man I'd known to remember the horrors of his past. Hell, he'd probably curse me until he ran out of words for bringing them up.

But at least he'd be himself to do so.

"Then do you remember the night Amalie stole it all? The way she spotted you when you were returning home from helping your neighbor deliver a calf? Do you remember how she demanded you join her, and how you thought her a madwoman? That was until she set fire to your village, her soldiers trapping everyone in their homes where they burned alive. Then, oh then, you begged her to stop. To let you join her. But she wouldn't. She said she wanted to teach you a lesson first."

He'd gone still as I spoke.

Praying he'd forgive me, I dug deeper for everything I recalled of what he'd told me about that night. He was the oldest of us. The one who'd been imprisoned by Amalie the longest, and I knew he buried his past behind a shield of humor and modernity, embracing whatever dialect and fashion was current to the world, if only to keep himself from remembering the time in which he'd first lived.

Not that I suspected he ever could. Some pain could never be buried no matter how much time went by. It only

146

waited for something to sweep the topsoil of your life aside and dredge the agony back into the light.

I'd never intended to do such a thing to him, but if this was working…

"Do you remember when she started in on your family?" I persisted though everything in me rebelled against torturing him this way. "How your sister screamed, at least until Amalie ripped her throat out? How even your stoic father cried to watch his daughter's life fade from her eyes? Your nephews, your brothers, your own mother. All of them dead at the queen's hand. And do you remember how Amalie smeared you with their blood and told you it was *your* fault they had to die?"

I couldn't even tell if he was breathing any longer.

"And do you remember how Amalie kept your niece alive, telling the child that her beloved uncle was going to drink blood and crave it? That you would become the same creature as her, the one who killed your family?"

I ached for him. I knew the girl had survived. Amalie sent the child fleeing into the night, all alone, letting her live to spread the word of how Ulysses had become a monster. Using that child, she'd stripped away from him any hope of returning to his past life, because anyone who heard the girl's story would have killed him on sight.

"Gods, brother, does none of this stir your memory? What of those first decades with the queen, when you begged her to let you die? Do you recall even *one* thing of who you were? Who *we* were, as the centuries went on?" Sorrow pressed down on me, but still I kept speaking, the words coming now like I'd opened a vault and all the past was tumbling out. "Do you recall how it felt when she bound you to Asher or Liam or me? The way it felt like your mind was collapsing and yet expanding. The way you said it made the torture worse and yet more bearable, because even if you wouldn't wish your hell on anyone, now you also weren't alone. Do you remember how strangely *right* it felt for the four of us to be connected to each other? More than Amalie ever seemed to know."

Shivers ran over my skin at the memory. Of everything Amalie ever did, only binding me to the others hadn't felt like a violation. I knew she'd intended it to be so. She'd wanted to make our torment worse—preventing us from escaping pain even when we were not the one being tortured. But it was solace in Hell. A lifeline in a sea of agony. A gift of brothers when I'd never had any before.

"Remember," I implored him, drawing out memory after memory until I barely knew what I was saying—only that I couldn't stop if I ever hoped to reach him. "When they built the Taj Mahal. When the Empire State Building rose above New York. When we sailed from England to Australia, all because you were angry at the way they were shipping people off to that continent. You wanted to help them, you said. And then we ended up trying to help the indigenous inhabitants instead. Do you remember?" My heart ached. "All those years, those centuries. The way we fought and the cities we saved and the promises we made. Remember how we defied his darkness, and the way the light shone on the cliff at her final sunrise, the ocean crashing beneath us and—"

His eyes snapped to me, and I cut off, startled. What had I been saying? Cliff? Sunrise? I didn't know those memories.

They weren't mine.

But everything of the man I'd known was in that shocked gaze.

A whisper carried through my mind, a woman's voice speaking words just beyond what I could hear, and in an instant, my heart broke. I'd missed that sound. I'd longed to hear it again, even if I couldn't recall ever having heard it before in my life. And even though I spoke dozens of languages, I couldn't understand what she was saying.

Ulysses' eyes widened.

Alarm shot through me. "Do you know those memories, brother? Of... of the cliff? The sun and..." Pain twisted inside me like a distant howl of agonized loss, but I couldn't understand why. "And someone who died?"

Why did I feel like it was more than that?

The whisper grew into a murmur, and I gasped at the sound. I *knew* this. But I couldn't recall—

Voices carried from outside the door, but I was barely able to concentrate on them. Grief and joy were choking me in equal measure, and I didn't even understand why.

What was happening to me?

I fought to make myself focus. "Can you fight him, brother? Come back to us?"

Whatever life there'd been in Ulysses' eyes was already fading, and I wanted to break something from fury over it.

"Fight, Ulysses! Please! I know you can come back to yourself if you just—"

The door opened.

I fell silent, shuddering at the desperation pounding

through me. Amalie sauntered into the room, her blood-red skirt swaying.

In their shackles, my hands curled into fists with sudden rage. She'd stolen so much. Corrupted so much.

Been corrupted, when she was more than this.

I faltered, confused by my own thoughts again. More than what?

"Ah, there you are, Ulysses," she said. "Visiting your stubborn friend, yes?"

She smiled, and my skin crawled. With every passing day, the strange shift in the face she now wore continued, making it appear more and more like the visage I remembered from centuries ago, even if none of the woman's features appeared to physically change. But a twist of red lips here, a lift of a dark eyebrow there, and it was as if I looked into the face of the monster who'd tortured me for years. After not too much longer, I'd wager this face would cease to resemble any previous photographs, all without her features actually altering in any discernible way.

The effect was chilling.

"I have a present for you today, Gideon. I've been playing with them for weeks, but I think it'd be more entertaining now to bring you in on the fun."

Ice spread through me. Had she captured Asher, Liam, or Wren, and I hadn't known?

She gestured over her shoulder, and a pair of rabids came into the room, setting immediately to unfastening me and locking the collar Amalie insisted upon around my throat.

I ignored them, my attention on Ulysses as he

shrugged away from the wall. Whatever I'd seen in his eyes was gone now. Only ice remained.

But I wouldn't let it continue that way. While the rabids hauled me away, I swore one thing to myself. No matter what strangeness had overtaken us moments ago, no matter what it took now, I'd find a way to reach him again.

Because if nothing else, I'd learned something invaluable.

My friend was still in there.

17

____

ULYSSES

In the darkness, there was only the voice hunting me, riding the wind like a monster from a nightmare.

And I couldn't fucking wake up.

I'd run through the tunnels of my mind for what felt like eternity, and the voice was always right behind me. Shadows swallowed everything in here, from the rough stone walls to the thread-thin trails of light woven through them, almost extinguished now. But the few glimpses of the outside world I saw past holes in the tunnels were too horrible for me to want to stick around. Death and destruction. Bodies bleeding out on the ground, and buildings burning. Crying people at my feet, pleading for mercy.

Right before my body attacked and killed them, drinking them down without a care.

"Uncle Ulysses..."

I cursed, trying to run faster. No matter how much the

voice sounded like my niece, I knew it couldn't be her.

Not with what she said.

"Why are you fighting him, Uncle Ulysses? He just wants to play a game. Come see."

I raced deeper into the darkness, grief and horror pulsing through me as rocks fell all around. My body was beyond my power; I couldn't control anything it said or did. But now the tunnels were starting to collapse, taking my memories with them. So little of me was left. Barely anything, really. I was starting to forget why I was even running.

"Don't you like the blood, Uncle Ulysses? It's so tasty."

Calliope would never have said that. She'd been good and innocent.

And Amalie shattered that.

I clung to the thought. Amalie was behind this somehow. I could barely even recall my own name half the time, but by the gods, I knew she had to be to blame.

"Should I tell you your past, then, *brother*?"

A new voice carried from far in the distance, fading in and out of hearing from beyond the shadows. I struggled to place it when so much was already gone.

Gideon, that was his name. I wanted to tell him to run. Being here wasn't safe.

I wasn't safe.

"Do you remember when she started in on your family?"

Gods, was this a trick too? He'd been my friend. Why was he trying to torture me? Hell was already in here with me, haunting me with the voices of the dead. I didn't need to be reminded of it.

Bad enough to watch my family die. Did he know about all the innocent people my body had killed now?

That *I* had killed?

"And do you remember how Amalie smeared you with their blood and told you it was *your* fault they had to die?"

I hated him. Sure—if this even *was* him—maybe he couldn't understand what was happening in here. The way Calliope's voice haunted me, entreating me to enjoy how my body drank the blood of those innocents, to revel in this nightmare and give in to the monster that had taken control of my mouth and limbs. The way I didn't even *want* to remember any longer; I only wanted to find a stake and run my heart through, just to make this end. But why the hell would Gideon think bringing up the worst moments of my life would be a good—

A whisper twisted through the darkness, different than Calliope's taunts. It wasn't Urlfeige, either. Hell, it wasn't even speaking words, not exactly. At least, none I understood.

Gideon's voice continued, undeterred. "All those years, those centuries. The way we fought and the cities we saved and the promises we made."

The whisper grew stronger, spreading through my mind like a murmur from a long-forgotten dream, soft and gentle yet somehow drowning out the hurricane that filled my world. It latched on to the memories he spoke of, as if it were cementing them in my mind, bastions against the onslaught. The words it spoke were familiar, but I couldn't understand them. And all around, the thread-thin trails of light in the stone walls grew brighter.

In spite of myself, I stopped running.

"Remember how we defied his darkness," Gideon continued. "And the way the light shone on the cliff at her final sunrise, the ocean crashing beneath us and—"

I looked over at him.

He cut off, staring at me.

I froze in shock. I could feel my own muscles, just a bit, and the light of reality was back, surrounding me, but it wasn't full of the dead this time.

It was still horrible.

Gideon was lashed to the wall, his body like a tapestry of wounds and blood. Had I been responsible for any of that? I couldn't remember. I'd run for so long, just trying to stay alive even if I couldn't stop my own body from the unspeakable things it did. But if I'd hurt him…

The murmur in my mind grew, comforting my shame and horror like the hand of a lover soothing you after a nightmare. I knew this voice, but I wasn't sure how. I'd missed it, though. Craved hearing it again, even if I hadn't remembered that until this moment. I'd spent lifetimes aching from fear that I might never hear it again. And now I only needed to reach out and take hold of it, and I could—

Calliope's laughter twisted around me, encircling me like a noose and pulling tight. "There you are."

More bindings wrapped me, trapping every inch of my mind. I'd been a fool to stop running.

"You don't get away that easily, Uncle Ulysses. He still wants to play."

I screamed as her laughter yanked me into the dark.

18

GIDEON

Like an entourage of Amalie's pets, the rabids, Ulysses, and I trailed her through the twists and turns of the cold hall beyond my cell. Snarls echoed in the distance, wild and hungry, the cries of newly turned vampires desperate to feed.

I hadn't heard any humans screaming in a long time.

"You're going to love this present I have for you," Amalie said, grinning back at me.

Flexing my hands in the shackles, I ignored her as I tried to restore sensation to my limbs. My body felt numb after so long hanging in chains, but as with every other time they brought me down these halls, I couldn't see any indication of a direction for escape anyhow. The gods only knew which corridor led outside and which led deeper into the complex.

And at the moment, damn her, I needed to know whom she'd captured.

At a door at the end of the hall, Amalie paused.

Drawing a ribbon from around her neck, she placed the key hanging from it into the lock and then gave me a smile over her shoulder. "I kept them alive especially for you."

My stomach turned sickly. Gods, what had she done?

Pushing open the door, she continued inside. The room beyond was dark, but when the rabids brought me in after her, a light flared to life.

Iron bars were driven straight into the concrete in two circles, and countless runes were chipped into their sides. The stench of burned flesh clung to the cold air. But it was the two people within those rough cages that sent ice rushing through my veins, a chill of horror boiled away swiftly by rage.

Friday and Barnaby were crumpled on the concrete floor, their clothes ripped and stained by blood. Their faces were haggard, as if they'd aged millennia in however long Amalie had held them here. Gray skin showed past the human illusion, as did the sharp bones of their natural forms. Shadows hung heavy on Friday's back as if her wings were too weak to lift her or to keep themselves hidden from this world.

But their eyes were only on each other. With one arm outstretched toward his wife, Barnaby was whispering something, and even though I couldn't hear his words, I could see the love on his face. He was reassuring her. Comforting her.

"Now, now," Amalie chided. "None of that."

She made a sharp motion, and the runes on the bars surrounding Barnaby flared to life as if lit by fire. The demon's back arched as a scream ripped from him, his body thrashing. Friday cried out, reaching toward him, only to recoil as the bars burned her and the smell of smoking flesh grew stronger on the air.

Amalie motioned again, and the fire inside the runes died. Barnaby collapsed to the ground again. Relief overwhelmed me to see he was still breathing.

"Do you like my present, Gideon?" Amalie grinned as if she were a child about to pull a trick. "Like I said, I've been playing with them for a while now, but I figure it's no fun to kill them on my own. Not when you could be my audience."

She turned toward Friday and Barnaby.

"Don't." The word ripped from me.

She glanced back. "Why not? You have something more fun for me? Like surrendering?"

Hate burned in my chest. In the end, she was always the same. Using anything that mattered to you as leverage. Object or animal or gods-damned sentient being. She didn't care what she had to hold hostage to bend you to her will.

I'd thought after all these centuries, the Sentinels and my eye were all I had left to lose. But I'd never been heartless, no matter how she'd tried to crush us.

No matter what he'd done.

I clenched my teeth against the strange thoughts still pressing at my mind, unexpected and unhelpful. I needed to focus if I was to save the demons.

Not that I could see a way other than giving her what she wanted.

"I'm bored, Gideon," Amalie said, a hint of petulant whine entering her voice, utterly theatrical. "You're all bloody, Ulysses is already mine, and I'm tired of watching humans scream and cry. They're all dead or turned now anyway. So give me what I want or I'm going to have to entertain myself some other—"

She cut off, alarm flashing across her face. The whisper in my mind swelled, distant but louder than before, lapping at the edges of my thoughts like a rising sea. Standing by the exit, Ulysses gave a low groan, his face twitching.

"What..." Amalie looked around briefly, and then her eyes locked on one wall as if staring at a point far beyond it. "That little *bitch*!"

With a furious shriek, she strode for the door. "Lock him to the wall!" she snapped over her shoulder at the rabids.

I barely noticed. A shiver ghosted over my skin like the barest touch of a hand on my cheek, my throat, my chest. Tears welled up inside me, unbidden, choking me with the urge to sob. But not with grief. Not entirely.

With joy because something I'd lost was returning. Something I'd loved was here at *long* last, stolen for eons but gone no more. She was out there. I only had to find her.

My eyes flashed around the room, seeing nothing different. It was as if only a second had passed. The rabid hauled on the chain, attempting to drag me toward the wall as Amalie had commanded. The other watched me from across the room, nothing but cruelty in her eyes.

I wanted nothing more than to cling to the whisper in my mind, but I had to focus now. Our survival depended on it.

Digging my feet in, I refused to move. The door was

open. Only two rabids guarded me. This was the best chance we'd have to get the hell out of here.

I shifted my weight, ready to throw off his grip and kill them both.

"Play nice," the woman warned, retreating as she spoke. "We know how to hurt the cranky old demons too."

Tugging a small object from her pocket, the woman pressed it as if it was a key fob. The runes flared to life again, and Friday and Barnaby screamed.

The woman grinned around her fangs and called to me over their cries. "I press this too hard and they'll die, Sentinel. You think you can kill me before I do that?"

Nearby, the man chuckled.

And Ulysses did nothing at all.

The demons' screams grew more tormented. Already their bodies began to shake and thrash as if they were being torn apart by some invisible force.

Curses in a dozen languages rolled through my mind.

I didn't resist as the other rabid fastened the chains to rings impaled in the wall. Still grinning, the woman released the device and threw an amused look at the demons as they sagged to the ground again. But when her eyes slid over to land on Ulysses, a hint of trepidation flashed across her face.

"Leave that one here," she said to the man.

Nodding, he followed her from the room, pulling the door closed behind them.

A clank sounded as the lock sealed us in. Inside my mind, the whispers continued, stronger now.

My heart ached to hear them, but I had to focus. "Friday. Barnaby. Are you okay?"

Clearly still in pain, the demons nodded.

My gaze slid to Ulysses, positioned by the wall like a robot put on pause. On my skin, the strange feeling of someone brushing their hand across me was still there, sinking farther inside like it wanted to enter my heart itself.

I closed my eye. I wanted this back, whatever it was, but given all of Urlfeige's tricks, that terrified me. I didn't know what was happening, so no matter how it pained me, I couldn't let this in deeper.

No, I needed to focus. I had to find us *all* a way out of here.

Because I wanted to make damn sure Amalie never harmed anyone ever again.

19

———

WREN

Dark liquid poured between my lips, tasting like water and burning like alcohol. Swallowing hard, I coughed a little and then lowered the cup, catching sight of Liam and Asher doing the same.

"What..." I coughed a second time. "What happens now?"

Motionless as a statue, Eden watched me and said nothing.

"Eden? What—" My brow twitched down, a weirdly cold feeling rolling through my body, like everything in me was falling and stretching backward at the same time. "What is—"

The twilight of the cottage grew darker. Had someone closed the curtains? I wasn't sure I still sat in the chair either. The falling sensation was everywhere around me now, but there wasn't any ground at the end of it. I was Alice tumbling down the rabbit hole, endlessly falling into an oblivion where down was up, and up was down, yet even those two directions were too solid and real for what was happening.

My thoughts blurred, and a whisper rose in my mind, same as it had weeks ago in the clinic. Words I couldn't understand twisted through my thoughts. A young woman was speaking to me, and her voice summoned up sights and sounds and scents that filled my head, each of them so alien and yet familiar.

Suddenly, I wasn't in Eden's cottage anymore.

I was *then*.

And I remembered.

20

TAU

*O*nce *upon a time, there was a kingdom...*

"Tauluria, where are you?"

I giggled as I ducked behind the large boulders at the edge of the farmland, only to peek back as the nursemaid strode farther down the path, still calling for me.

"I told you my pillow doll was more lifelike." Nialora's teasing whisper couldn't hide her own excitement at narrowly avoiding capture. Neither of us were supposed to be out of our family's fortress. But the angels had been painting the sky with color and song tonight, the music calling to us to come outside, come see.

How were we supposed to sleep through that?

"Only because *you* look like one," I teased my fraternal twin sister.

With a scoff, she shoved my shoulder, sending me toppling to the side, though humor glinted in her eyes. "You'll pay for that, you—"

She fell silent as brilliant light ghosted across the sky, green like grass and gold like the dawn. Our eyes fixed on it, and a low murmur of amazement left Nia. The angelic singing echoed in us, bringing a smile to my face. Of everyone in the fortress, only we and our mother could hear it.

But then, Mother *was* an angel, and we had enough of her blood in us to enable our hearts to resonate with their song.

"Beautiful," I whispered.

Nia murmured agreement. "Do you think Mother will let us join in when we're older?"

I bit my lip, hope bubbling up within me as the lights faded. "Maybe? If we practice really hard?"

She started to nod when a new light shot through the darkness, brilliant orange, coming closer with every second. "What... what is that?"

The world exploded into flame.

***

"And I'm telling you, we cannot withstand another winter like the last!" I turned away from my father's general, my skin broiling with the urge to scream my rage into the sky. We'd been fighting this war for so long, sometimes it seemed that was all there'd ever been. Ever since the fiery first night of their attack, our enemies had summoned everything from witches to demons to help them steal our land, and each day, more of us succumbed to starvation.

"Princess Tauluria, the people will simply have to

endure fewer rations. If they wish the war effort to sustain—"

A furious noise escaped me. "Sustain *what*? If everyone in these walls is dead, what *exactly* will your army be defending?"

Anger suffused his face. "As representative of your father during his absence, I have made my decision. The army will—"

"My father would *not* want this."

I spun on my heel, refusing to wait for more. Nia would have already made progress hiding supplies while I argued with the old man. Mother would too. The escape tunnels my father had secretly built into the fortress for his daughters and wife, years ago, made good hiding spaces away from the covetous hands of a general who saw more benefit in a war to defend scorched land than in saving the widows and orphans of that land from death.

Yet *he* was my father's representative, charged with "protecting us."

Like Mother couldn't defend herself. Like Nia and I hadn't spent every waking moment since childhood training to fight. Father knew that.

But still, he'd left that man in command during his absence.

Absence. I fought back a grimace. Was that what it was, truly? I'd heard the whispers—that he'd abandoned us all. That the good leader my people loved had betrayed them, taking soldiers we could have used to defend our lands and fleeing instead. I didn't believe it for a moment, but that didn't stop the whispers or the greed of his generals from growing.

I could only hope he'd be proud of what his wife and daughters had accomplished, in spite of everything.

But he'd been gone for years, and we only had rumors to go on for what he'd done in that time, each story more absurd and unlikely than the last. Meanwhile, we were besieged on all sides by enemies who sought to take our lands, all because we were at the crossroads of so many trade routes.

Father once told us he was leaving to seek allies to fight with us. That he'd come back with armies made of those allies who owed him, who were loyal.

I'd seen them. They were attacking us too.

The siren song of power was too great a lure.

Nia appeared at the corner of the hall, her pale eyes worried and her hands wringing one another.

I slowed, confused. "What's wrong?" I lowered my voice. "Did someone catch you hiding the—"

Her head shook quickly. "It's—"

A shriek came from beyond the turn. It sounded like Mother.

Instantly, Nia spun and took off back toward the sound. Panic flooding me, I raced after her.

Something crashed in the great hall. Nia tore through the door ahead of me. "Mother!"

"No, Nia, don't—"

My sister shrieked. Terror shooting through me, I charged in after her, yanking free the sword that was forever at my hip.

No one but my sister and mother was in the massive room. But Nia was on the floor, collapsed at our mother's feet. Mother stood over her, broad white wings spread across her daughter with the tips curled in a protective position. Radiant power shone from her, glowing gold across the stone columns and walls, yet there was nothing but horror on her face.

But I couldn't see why.

"Tau, get down!" Mother cried.

I dropped for the floor, but I couldn't move fast enough. Hands grabbed me, wrestling me back against a hard chest with a grip like stone.

"Hello, daughter."

Alarm shot through me, and I twisted. "Father?"

My eyes went wide, a choked noise escaping me. He didn't look a thing like the man I remembered, with his kind smile and his jovial laugh that brought joy to any who heard it. His eyes were dead and cold, and his skin was too. No kindness or mercy showed in his gaze, and as he smiled at me, his teeth were joined by fangs like a wild beast.

Terror made my muscles shake.

"Urlfeige," my mother pled. "I see only darkness around you, my love. What have you done?"

"I found the answer. They showed me the way. The *only* way."

"What?" Her eyes flashed between me and my father. "Please, beloved, let your daughter go. Let me speak to my people. The angels can help—"

"The ones who haven't turned against us, you mean. The ones who aren't aiding our enemies."

Pain showed on her face. "Let Tau *go*. Please. Don't—"

He yanked me back against him harder, and his hand tugged on my hair to pull my head to the side.

"No!" Mother screamed.

His fangs bit down on my neck. Leaping forward, Mother charged at us, but shadows swept down from the ceiling, swirling around us and slashing at her like they were alive.

Incredulity hammered at me for the shadows and my father *biting* me alike, but I had no time for it. Shifting my weight, I wrenched at his grip, attempting to break free of him.

His hold was impossibly strong.

Panic drummed a fast rhythm in my chest, but the beat was weakening. The angelic power in me was faltering under a strange darkness, like something was drowning it in mud. My limbs began to feel heavy, my body numb, but muscle memory made me twist the sword in my grip to slash at him.

The blade sliced his leg.

He merely chuckled against my neck and then withdrew his fangs from my throat. I tried to throw myself forward, desperate to get away from him and the shadows, but he only tore his teeth across his own wrist and then shoved it between my lips.

Blood filled my mouth.

I choked on it, still fighting to be free of him and this madness. The wounds on my neck still throbbed, my own blood pumping out of the injuries to soak my chest. Every second made the great hall grow darker and colder.

I blinked. Realizing that despite my darkening vision, I could see the room again, the swirling shadows gone. But Nia and Mother were nowhere to be seen.

The sword slipped from my grasp, hitting the stone

floor with a distant *thunk*. Words reached my ears, muffled and nearly meaningless now.

"—angel took the girl, my lord."

"It's no matter." My father's voice rumbled from above where he still held me suspended in his arms while the world faded. "We'll find them. And I have this one. She'll be enough."

———

When I woke again, nothing in my life was ever the same.

Mostly because it had ended that day.

In the time that followed, I came to understand what manner of monster he'd turned himself, his army, and me into. We were what we were because of his quest. He'd sought help from everyone he met, trying to protect us, all to no avail. His mission seemed a failure until, in the rocky wastes of a desert with most of his company dead, he found them.

The beings in the spaces between worlds where even the gods feared to tread. Creatures no human was ever meant to meet. I heard how they'd offered him power and transformed him into a new thing, a monster with no real life of its own, sustaining itself instead on blood and death. And all so that he could be our savior, defending his people from any who would seek to harm us.

He even believed it.

But although he'd bitten me just as he had all his soldiers who'd survived his quest—transforming them into creatures like himself, with bodies that shifted between shadow and form with barely a thought—I was still nothing like them.

My heart was still human.

And unlike every other one of his creations, the sun's touch didn't burn me.

My father cared nothing for the former, determined to break it out of me, but the latter had always been his goal in turning me. He'd suspected my mother's blood would make me unique among his creatures, and it thrilled him to find that the legacy of angels protected me from the sun. Within days of my turning, he was trying to force me to turn others and build him an army even more powerful, unrestrained by sunlight. But I refused to bite anyone, and even when he stole my blood—slashing me with a blade and sending his servants to collect what spilled—it wouldn't pass my protection on to them.

Oh, he raged at that.

As time crept on, I fought however I could to resist him. He tried endlessly to compel me to feed, believing the more I did, the more my resistance to harming the innocent would weaken—and ultimately bring me around to serving him. When I wouldn't bite a person, he brought blood in goblets and bowls, commanding me so strongly, it drove his servants to the floor in terror. But still I refused. His people pinned me down, forcing blood between my lips, but I would only make myself throw up as much as I could later.

My body grew weak. My lungs and heart stopped. Hunger gnawed at me ceaselessly, riding me until I thought I'd go mad. But I swore to myself I wouldn't give in. The fact he'd once been the father I believed in broke my heart, but I couldn't let that sway me. I wouldn't make him an army or take someone's life. Not like he'd taken mine. I'd die first.

And then they came.

At first, all I heard were the screams.

From my seat near the window of the bedroom that was my prison, I didn't look away from the thread I'd been dismantling from my blanket. My father had used his dark magic to block every exit from this room, from the slit windows to the secret tunnels. I couldn't even depress the combination of stones needed to open the hidden door.

But after so many years of trying, I'd given up on escaping that way. I'd given up on almost any escape, really.

Except a final one.

The screams grew worse. Closer. My father would certainly bring me blood soon. He'd failed so far to make me harm anyone or to twist my unique abilities to his own ends. But every day my battle with hunger grew worse, and I could feel my control slipping.

I closed my eyes briefly, ordering myself to focus on the rope I planned to weave. Over the years, many humans had tried attacking the fortress. Some made it to the walls. Some even to the courtyard. But none survived. My father had achieved all he'd ever wanted in securing our "safety," and now anyone who challenged his lands died horribly as food for his soldiers or was turned, becoming one of them.

He sent the latter group back to their people, where they unleashed his vengeance, killing even those they loved. Whole villages had been destroyed now. Entire regions too, their people and their stories gone forever.

But still, the humans fought, brave to the end.

Still, they died.

The screams faded. My hands shook, and I dropped the thread, curling my fingers into fists as I resisted the urge to scream too. It wouldn't do any good, and it wouldn't save anyone. But if I finished weaving my rope laden with fragments of metal from my old armor and jewelry, and propelled myself with enough force from the beams on the ceiling...

The damage would be painful, at least at first. But it might be enough to make this end.

New shouts rose. Raw howls of pain that were closer still and didn't have the horrible sound of mortal death I'd come to know far too well. Confused, I rose to my feet, but when I reached the window, all I could do was stare.

"What?" I whispered.

Tumbling to the ground and writhing on the dirt, his soldiers were clutching their throats as their skin turned to ash and began to crumble away. Around them, humans lay, their throats torn out from the vicious feeding of soldiers who enjoyed watching their victims suffer. Blood still crusted the soldiers' mouths.

Which were decaying first.

"Oh, gods." Horrified respect for the humans spread through me. "They poisoned themselves. They—"

A thud came from the other side of the tunnel exit. The stone wall swung back.

Four enormous warriors strode into the room, savage blades carved with runes and spells in their grasp. Their bodies were made of muscle and scars, their stances radiating the threat of death. How they'd found the secret tunnel made no sense to me, but as one, they stalked forward, weapons at the ready.

In my human life, I would have seen men who made my body burn with desire and trepidation. Now I only saw my salvation.

If I could resist the compulsion to feed.

Quickly, I made myself scramble in retreat until my back hit the wall. "Please." I dug my fingers into the stone to keep myself from lunging at the human men. "Throw your blades. Kill me. Now, before my father finds you here."

They paused.

"Now, damn you!" I could feel my fangs trying to emerge, my starved body fighting my will not to feed. "Isn't that why you're here?"

The one nearest to me straightened slightly, his knife lowering. "Yes."

"Good! Then—"

"But we came to kill a rabid beast."

A ragged noise escaped me. They were staring like they'd never seen anything like me in their lives—a delay that might just cost them theirs.

"That's what I am," I ground out. "A beast who needs to die. So for the fucking sake of the gods, *destroy me* before he—"

My bedroom door crashed open. My father and his soldiers charged in.

New terror gripped me. They'd kill the humans, soaking my bedroom floor with their blood, and I wouldn't be able to stop myself from diving in to join the meal. For me to feed at all would be victory for him.

But to do that while losing my best shot at making this end...

I threw myself between my father and the warriors, my body turning from form to shadow and back. Before he could reach them, I struck the four men and threw them backward across the room.

My father and his creatures pulled up short, staring at me. I bared my fangs, not having to fake the ferocity in my voice as I snarled, "*Mine.*"

Satisfaction glinted in my father's eyes, but caution too. "Their blood is poisoned, daughter. I will bring you a different meal."

The sound that came from me was more animal than human. "*Mine!*"

A cold smile pulled at his lips. "Then allow us to chain them for you to enjoy later, and I will bring you a drink we know is safe now. If you've truly decided to stop starving yourself, that is."

I trembled. If I drank, he won. If I let them die, he won. I looked back at the warriors behind me, anguish in my eyes.

Questions filled theirs. I'd confused them, but it didn't matter. If they lived, they could finish their mission and end this. Maybe I could even give them enough information about the fortress and my father that they'd be able to escape as well.

But meanwhile, whoever had been sacrificed for the meal he wanted to bring me? They were already gone.

Drawing up all the resolution I could, I turned back. "Agreed."

Victory filled his eyes.

Gods, I hated him. And to think I'd once only wanted his approval...

At a snap of his fingers, several of his soldiers rushed away, returning only a moment later with chains.

And blood.

"Then let us see you drink, daughter."

My hands shook, but I took the goblet. I fought not to look at it, but instinctively, my eyes twitched down.

I froze. Only a tiny amount of blood filled the bottom, barely enough to sustain me a day.

"That is merely a snack," my father said as if reading my expression. "Human blood cleans itself well, after all. These fools will be safe for you to drink soon." He leaned toward me. "If any still live in a week, they will wish you'd given them the gift of death."

My fingers tightened on the goblet. *Then I have one week to get them free*, I replied silently.

And to make sure I died instead.

Closing my eyes, I swallowed down the blood, despising myself for how much my body craved it. In only a moment, my heart fluttered to life and my lungs drew in a shallow breath. As I let the goblet fall, his soldiers grabbed the men, disarming them and tying them to the stone pillars of my room. When they finished, my father walked over and bent slightly, touching his fingers to each restraint and whispering words I couldn't hear.

A sheen passed across the bindings, glistening sickly green in the firelight. He smiled as he straightened and turned back to me. "So you are barred from breaking them."

He and his soldiers left the room.

I shivered with rage. But it faded to desperation as I looked at the warriors. Despite what he'd said, I still rushed over to them, hauling on their bindings.

Nothing budged, but the metal burned my hands, making me hiss with pain as I recoiled. Next, I went hunting for a weapon, but nothing was left in the room.

"Princess," said one of them, a massive man with a scar across his eye as if someone had sought to take it out.

"I will get you out of this," I promised, barely sparing him a glance.

"Your sister misses you."

I froze. "What did you say?"

"Princess Nialora. She misses you."

"She's alive?"

He nodded. "Your mother too, last we knew. Her people called her back to them after she fled this place. But your sister remains. She gave us the location of the tunnels." He paused. "And she told us what happened to you."

Anguish and longing tangled inside me, so strong I suddenly couldn't breathe again. I'd missed them so much, but as the years went by and nothing changed, I'd worried maybe...

"She begged us to only kill you if we had no other

choice," said another whose skin was pale like all life had been drained from him. I knew some would think he was cursed because of that. But his eyes held the intensity of a trained warrior and his rich voice sent warmth pooling through me in a way I'd never thought I'd feel again. On its heels came a hunger for his blood, though, lapping at the edges of my mind like a toxic sea.

The combination terrified me.

"You don't," I whispered, my voice cracking. "He made me a monster."

"But not, I think, like he wanted you to be," said another, a discerning look in his eye, like he could see all the possibilities laid out before him, and he knew he'd picked the right one. He'd been the first to speak when they came in here, the first to lower his weapon, and something about him made me think he was their leader.

I shook my head at his words, the pressure of all their gazes burning me. "Doesn't matter." I turned my attention back to their bindings.

Nothing worked. Not that night. Not the next day or the next. No matter what tools I used, no matter how I pulled on the restraints, my hands burned and bleeding out what little blood I had left, nothing could break them free.

But every day, my father came, a servant following him to bring the men food. He'd smile in a way that reminded me of a crocodile and tell me how much time was left until—by my fangs or his—they would die.

"Don't listen," Tyrkuren murmured as the door shut.

I couldn't bring myself to nod. Over the past few days, I'd come to know them better. Tyrkuren bore the scars, while the pale one was called Seterios. The first one who'd spoken to me when they came here was Zerick, their leader, and the last was Mal, a man with quick humor that belied his haunted eyes. They were sworn as blood brothers, and for years they'd fought to keep humanity safe from my father and his monsters.

Everything I wished I could have done, if only I hadn't been one of them.

My eyes closed. I was no closer to freeing the warriors—or myself. But it was sunset on the last night before their time was up, and when sunrise came... they'd die.

I yanked on the manacles again, my hands bloody and weeping but long since dulled to the pain.

"Princess," Tyrkuren pressed. "Please."

My head shook. "I have to..."

"Please."

A sob pressed on my chest as I sank down next to them, these men who'd become the closest thing I had to friends over the brief week they'd been here.

"You tried, Princess," Zerick said. "And we thank you."

"For what? Prolonging your suffering?" I squeezed my eyes shut, and my voice was barely a whisper as I said, "You were supposed to kill *me*."

Silence hung heavy in the room. I shoved the grief back, opening my eyes. "I can't free you. I'm sorry. I should have just helped you escape or—"

"We all know that wouldn't have worked," Zerick interrupted gently. "We were here on a mission, and your father arrived too soon."

"But now, he'll..."

"You could end it for us first," Tyrkuren said when I trailed off.

I looked over at him in alarm. Despite his scars, his expression was gentle. "I-I can't—"

"Escaping him is mercy, Princess," Seterios told me. "And we knew what the cost could be from the start."

I retreated from them, my motionless heart still managing to ache. That I knew they were right only made it worse. But to let my father finally make me a killer on top of it all—

"Or we choose another way," Mal said.

Confusion fractured my pain. "What?"

He looked at the others, and some silent understanding appeared to pass between them. One by one, they nodded.

"You turn us," Mal said.

A horrified sound escaped me. "*What?*"

Mal's mouth tightened, while Seterios sighed and Tyrkuren turned his eyes to the sliver of a window, where the sky was growing darker now that the horizon had swallowed the sun.

"You are not like him, Princess," Zerick said. "And perhaps your blood—your ancestry—is why."

My head shook. "But it didn't work. He tried to force me to—"

"Perhaps that's *why* it didn't," Seterios interrupted. "Force will never give the same result as consent. You did not agree for him to use your blood that way, and so he failed." His pale eyes were solemn. "You have power too."

My mouth moved, and when I found my voice, it came

out shaky. "But I don't want to live like this. I... I thought you could kill me before—"

"If we survive and become like you," Zerick said, his voice kind, "we'll return. We'll get you out of here."

Trembling gripped me. To leave... to see my sister or mother again...

I shook my head. "But I'll still be a monster. I'll still be what he made me."

Zerick made a compassionate, incredulous sound, like he couldn't believe my words. "You don't see yourself, Princess. You see him and his soldiers. We see *you*. We've been here a week, and through every second of it, you've been in pain—for us. To spare us, no matter how hungry you clearly are. And not once have you faltered or even flashed a fang in desire to feed."

He reached out, taking my hand, his skin so warm against mine. "You're not a monster. You're an incredible, beautiful woman with breathtaking control and empathy, no matter what you've suffered. You're nothing he made. And you can be free."

Tyrkuren turned from watching the window. "He could return at any time. Either we risk this now, or he will make us like his creations."

"If he doesn't just torture us until we beg to die," Mal added with a smile like a man standing before an executioner.

My stomach churned with horror.

But hunger was there too.

"It's this or far worse, Princess," Seterios said, tension creeping into his voice. "You are *not* the same as him. You have mercy. If this is what is left to us, then let us join you rather than become like the beasts that destroyed our homes."

"Unless it doesn't *work*," I whispered desperately.

His brow rose and fell. "You're our only hope that it ever could."

My eyes turned to the window. So little time left, and every second I delayed was a gamble. Because Tyrkuren was right. At any moment, my father could decide he'd waited long enough and return to drink them dry.

Or make them into his monsters.

"Who first?" I whispered.

"Me," Zerick said before the others could speak. "In case it takes a try or two to get it right."

I squeezed my eyes shut, wishing I still had tears to cry. But it wouldn't change this anyway.

I shifted closer to him. The warmth of his skin stoked the fires of hunger and need inside me. Digging my nails into my palm, I focused on every ounce of humanity and compassion I possessed, praying it would carry through to them all.

"I'm sorry," I whispered.

My fangs pierced his throat.

When he found the four warriors dead in my room, my father was exultant. Full to the point of nausea on their blood, I sat on the floor nearby, barely able to look at him as he stood over me, pride and satisfaction on his face.

"Now you understand, daughter. Now you know what it is to embrace who you truly are."

As his people started toward the bodies, I bit back a noise of protest. I didn't want a single monster to touch them or take them away. But I knew I had to allow it. They'd dump their bodies in the pit where my father's people disposed of all the rest of their meals' remains, and maybe that'd give the men a chance. But if he knew I'd tried to turn them...

I kept my hands clasped in front of me. I'd cleaned my blood from their lips before he arrived. There should be nothing left on the warriors to lead him to think he could now make me turn others.

If this had even worked...

"Would you like to come join us in the dinner hall?" my father offered.

My head shook. "I'm not hungry... anymore." The words felt as if they were being ripped from me, but he only smiled.

"Later, then."

I made myself nod.

The door shut. Tears welled in my eyes as I hugged my legs to my chest and waited to see whether I'd saved those good men or damned them.

It took three nights.

I was sitting on my bed, watching angelic light dance across the sky beyond my window, when the stones on my wall moved again, the secret escape route opening. The four warriors walked into my room dressed in cloaks with their knives once again at their sides. Everything in me stopped, waiting to see if anything of their former selves remained.

Crossing to my bedside, Zerick offered me his hand. Warily, I took it, letting him draw me to my feet.

His eyes were kind as he smiled at me. "Now it's our turn to set you free."

Near the exit, Tyrkuren nodded toward the tunnel. "He barred this end against you opening it. He only barred the other end against humans."

"Sloppy," Mal added with mock disapproval, grinning around his fangs.

"We need to go," Seterios said, ignoring him. "They'll notice the guards in the supplies room are gone soon." From beneath his cloak, he withdrew a long, slender sword and offered it to me. "Your sister once told us you know how to use this."

The hilt felt like it had come home to me when it touched my hand. Gripping it tightly, I threw a look around my room, my prison, but there was nothing I wanted to take. Nothing here that mattered to me at all.

Life waited beyond these walls.

I strode past Tyrkuren, bracing myself as I passed through the opening and into the tunnel. But with the door open now, no magic bit at me. Grinning, I started running, the four men racing after me. My feet flew across the stones, moving with more speed than I'd known I could achieve.

At every step, the warriors were with me.

A guard appeared at the end of the tunnel, alarm on his face as he saw us charging at him. Before he could shout a warning, knives flew past me, striking him dead. Turned to dust, my father's creation crumbled in our wake.

And then we were beyond the fortress walls, all the night open before us.

Together, we took to the sky.

Once upon a time, there was a rebellion...

We were nothing he'd made, and everything I could have dreamed. Some humans thought us chosen by the gods, others called us the spawn of the underworld. But together, we saved cities and defied my father's armies.

The princess and her loyal Sentinels.

I never cared about names or titles. The mission that brought the warriors to me was mine as well, and the change my blood had wrought in them went deeper than I ever imagined. My angelic side was long buried beneath what my father had done, but traces of it still flowed through me, and the power I'd forced into my bite and blood when I turned the warriors had linked all of us together. We knew when one of us was hurt or needed help, when there was danger and when we were safe. It'd even given them my protection from the sun. Early on, I told the warriors I'd find some way to set them free of the link to me. I didn't want even the *chance* I'd created slaves like my father made.

But they refused. I'd given them a gift, they said. A way to be more formidable against our enemies. A way to fight better as a team. Additionally, even though I was adept with weapons and hand-to-hand combat, this way they would always know if I was okay.

And more than that.

Bit by bit, I fell in love with each of them, and them with me. Our need for each other quickly moved past sharing blood so that we'd never need to feed on an innocent, all the way to sharing a bed. Mornings found me wrapped in their arms, sated and more content than I'd ever dreamed I could be.

But it couldn't last.

One autumn night, my father's soldiers found us. We fled, and I cried out hoping my sister and the angels would come to help, but there wasn't time. My father's forces cut us off, leaving us completely surrounded with our backs to the endless ocean.

And no way out.

"Surrender," he called, all his army arrayed behind him and his power rolling across the barren terrain like a cloak of pure night.

"Never." I gripped my sword, the power I'd grafted to it and the warriors' blades over the years thrumming in my hand, making it glow against the dark.

His lips curled. "Then die."

Dark magic rushed at us.

Calling upon every scrap of my angelic heritage still inside me, I extended my own power around us, barely sheltering us in time. The impact sent me stumbling, and I choked on pain as his magic chewed at my defenses like a thousand tiny teeth of monsters.

I'd never been stronger than him, not when I was his prisoner. Not now, and I knew it. What he'd done had buried my angelic side.

But I'd be damned if I went down without a fight.

My warriors grabbed me as the seething magic around

us bit deeper into my defenses. Love and strength poured through the connection between us, and I clung to it, fighting to keep his power at bay.

Through the snarling shadows and hungry night, my father strode toward me, stopping at the very edge of where my gifts held back the dark.

And he smiled.

Throwing his hand out toward us, he sent waves of darkness rushing across my defenses, all of them twisting and teeming like snakes and eels come to life. A profound emptiness radiated from them, and horror gripped me.

That wasn't just dark magic. That was power from beyond the worlds. It'd transformed him once.

What would it do if it struck us now?

Fear gave me fuel, pouring more power into the shield around my warriors, my Sentinels, my loves, and I screamed as the creatures raked at it. The damage blazed through me like a blast wave of fire, scouring me as I fought to keep the beasts from touching the four men with me.

The creatures' teeth chewed at my magic. At my essence. Through them, my father's power ripped into me like he was trying to flay me alive. I couldn't breathe, couldn't feel my heart beat. Everything in me was being scoured away.

Down to the angel deep inside.

I screamed, the golden light of my mother's heritage surging up as best it could against his onslaught.

To save the ones I loved.

Light exploded from me, burning back the dark. My father howled as it struck him, his body turning to ash and smoke. His darkness melted away like fog in the sun while his body crumbled and the last of my strength swept the battlefield.

And then there was only silence.

Shaking hard, I caught myself with one hand on the dead grass, fighting to keep from collapsing fully to the ground. My body felt hollow and raw, like I'd been emptied of everything inside. But in an instant, Zerick was there, gathering me up quickly and holding me close. Arrayed before us, my father's creatures stared, making no move to attack.

Seterios, Tyrkuren, and Mal took a step toward them, blades drawn.

The creatures recoiled, wide-eyed and looking around as if unsure what to do now that my father was gone.

Sunlight pierced the horizon behind us. Shouts broke out among the army, and in an instant, they were fleeing as fast as they could in the opposite direction.

Tyrkuren scoffed.

Holding me close, Zerick paid them no attention. "You did it." He smiled at me. "You defeated—"

Pain gripped me, and I cried out.

Horror suffused Zerick's face, and I looked down.

Oh, gods, I was burning in the sunrise. Everything I had had gone into that blast.

None of my protection from the sun remained.

"Shield her!" he shouted.

Tyrkuren was already turning to shadow, sweeping around us to protect me as Seterios did the same.

"There's a cave!" Mal shouted from the air. "Quarter mile that way!"

"Not like this, Tau," Zerick begged, scrambling to his feet, bringing me with him. "Just hang on. Just..."

My body couldn't last. Reaching up as my hands began to turn to ash, I touched Zerick's cheek as his anguished eyes met mine.

"I'll see you again," I whispered as the light began to fade.

It took thousands of years.

But I was right.

21

WREN

My eyes opened. Wood slats crossed the ceiling above me. Herbs hung from the rafters, and the soft sound of birdsong was somewhere nearby.

Confusion furrowed my brow. I wasn't lying on a cliff-side, the sun burning me. I wasn't in Zerick's arms. No, this was... else. Other. A different time.

A different life.

And I was Wren.

I tried to sit up, and everything in my body protested the motion, but slowly, the aches faded. As a breath pressed from my chest, I glanced around.

My eyes landed on two men lying on the wood floor as well.

A sob left me, and before I even registered the impulse, I was scrambling over to them. Their eyes were closed, but their chests moved, and as I pressed a hand to them, they stirred like they'd been asleep.

Zerick's eyes opened.

No, not Zerick. Asher. That was his name now.

"Tau?" he whispered.

Gasping against another sob, I managed a smile.

His hand rose, taking my cheek, and his brow twitched down. "Wren," he said like he was placing my name.

I nodded.

At his side, Seterios made a noise of discomfort, and Asher looked over, alarm flashing across his face. "Set—Liam. We're safe. Don't attack."

Liam's eyes opened, darting around the room, and everything in his body language was predatory. But after a moment, he grimaced, the tension fading slightly, and he looked over at us.

The discomfort on his face cleared into relief when he saw me.

I reached out to him, and he took my hand, squeezing it hard.

A soft sound to my left drew my attention, and I looked over to find a woman with long brown hair watching us warily. She was seated on a small wooden chair, a table of crystals and other small items at her side.

And I knew her. She was—I racked my mind for the name—Eden.

"What did you see?" she asked.

I eyed her, weighing how much to say, but she'd helped us. Helped me, back when I was dealing with the other one. Amalie.

The life that went so wrong.

Shivers rolled through me as my mind reeled, trying to make sense of all the new-old information. I remembered being Tau, back in a time so distant archeologists thought humans hadn't even mastered huts—and how wrong was *that*? I remembered being Amalie too, the one who would have given anything for her father's approval, who had been so warped and twisted by a lifetime of bad choices and worse treatment that she rejected any whisper of Tau's soul because she saw only weakness there. Yet she'd still been driven by a compulsion to find the Sentinels and restore *something* of what had been. She'd reawakened pieces of their gifts from their past lives—protection from the sun most of all—and extended it back to herself. But with her power, she'd held their pasts and even the spirit of Tau herself at bay, while smothering any trace of compassion or humanity inside herself.

She'd made herself so like our father. He would've been proud.

No... not ours. Tau's. Back when we were her.

I shook my head, working to orient myself. The solid floor beneath me and the scents of herbs hanging from the rafters were grounding, and I rubbed my hands across my thighs, centering myself in my own body. What I'd seen was imprinted on me, like a truth bound to every cell and molecule of my being. But I was Wren. Yes, I'd *been* Tauluria. That'd been real too, once upon a time. But I was still Wren.

Eden was waiting.

"Memories," I said.

"Another life," Asher added.

Eden's brow twitched up.

"We were..." I glanced at Asher and Liam. "We were together. But different."

I told her what I'd seen.

Eden nodded when I finished. "Interesting."

There was an odd note in her voice, and I wasn't sure what to make of it.

"That wasn't all," Asher said.

I gave him a confused look.

"After you..." He cleared his throat, pain flashing over his face as he looked at me. "*After*. The vampires who'd been there weren't the same. They had compassion. Humanity. They were the people they'd once been."

My brow twitched down. "Dormants."

He nodded. "The first ones. Over the years, we worked with them to make the cure that stops a newly turned person from being rabid." A thoughtful look crossed his face. "Everyone always knew it was an old remedy. These days, I mean. We just didn't know how old." He drew a breath. "It's only effective right when they're first turned, though, not once they've fed and gone full rabid. No one else was ever able to do what you did that day."

I stared at him. "But you... you were okay after that, yeah? You and—" I glanced at Liam. "And the others?"

The two men shared a brief look. "What happened affected us too," Asher admitted. "Weakened us. We made it a few more decades before..." He shrugged. "I don't think any of us really minded, though. It wasn't the same with you gone."

My heart ached for them, and I reached out, squeezing his hand, wishing I knew how to fix wounds from thousands of years ago.

"If you created the dormants," Eden said. "Then that might explain what's happened now."

Still gripping Asher's hand, I turned to her. "What do you mean?"

"Because you're the link."

"Huh?"

"In your previous life, you made the dormants. While you apparently never connected to them the way you did with the Sentinels, *something* of you spread to them all the same. And they created the cure for a rabid's bite from that. It's magic, but ancient, and it's kept countless vampires from becoming monsters." She nodded to herself like she was fitting the pieces into place inside her head. "He made vampires. You made vampires who could still access their own souls. And from that, a cure was made based upon what you were and what you did. But he can't override that. He doesn't have any of that angelic nature that would enable him to do so."

"But..." I gave her a confused look. The problem with her theory seemed obvious. "He has Amalie."

"And if I had to guess, I'd say they thought she was going to be enough. But they were wrong."

I looked away, something in me suspecting she was right. Back in Cincinnati, the rabids had left me to turn to dust when they ripped Amalie from my mind. They wouldn't have done that if they thought they needed *me* alive at all.

Or, rather, Tau.

I grimaced. My head was starting to hurt just from trying to keep this all straight.

"Whatever spell he's cast is *massive*," Eden continued as if talking to herself. "It's almost certainly drawing on the empty realms to sustain itself, and given what you describe, it probably took him this long to regain enough strength after that attack to even try it. But if it were to operate at full potential?"

"Yeah...?" I asked when she trailed off.

"Global. It would have to be. I can't imagine he's going to leave a single vampire free."

Shivers crawled over my skin.

"But," she continued. "He still needs Tau's essence to be present to override the dormants' control of themselves. When you and Amalie were both at the clinic, his spell could spread like wildfire. But each of you on your own? She can't do it, and you only affect those right in front of you." Eden gave me a pointed look. "You're still resisting him, and she's not enough like the princess for it to be effective."

A breath left me. I'd fought him at the clinic, back when his power tried to crawl inside my head. I'd burned him out, even if I hadn't understood what I was doing at the time.

But it hadn't been enough, not to keep his spell from affecting any dormants near me.

Pollen, pollen carries the bumblebee...

"Can you stop it?" I asked Eden in a rush. "Give me a pendant or a potion or something that will keep any dormants around me from—"

"Against something like this?" Grimacing, she looked away, her brow shrugging. "It's the empty realms. My power..."

She trailed off, something flickering over her face that I couldn't quite read. It looked like pain—and a lot of defeat.

Her head shook. "I'm sorry."

I closed my eyes briefly, not sure how to feel. She'd helped us today. We had more answers now. But God, I'd wanted all the rest of this to be easy. Simply come here, get some kind of magic, and presto. No more ancient vampire boogeyman.

Who was still after me, all these millennia later.

My skin crawled. "It's okay. Thank you for all you've done."

The words barely seemed to mollify her. "Be careful, all right? Please. He wanted Amalie to have this because she will *gladly* let him destroy everything Tau made that day. And if he and Amalie get their hands on you, I can't imagine they don't have a plan to drain that power from you somehow."

I shivered, but I nodded.

Pushing to her feet, she waited for us to rise. As we made our way to the door, she began fiddling with the crystals and trinkets on her table again, her expression growing distant.

My steps slowed. "Eden, are you sure you're okay?"

She flashed me a smile that didn't make me feel even a tiny bit better. "Fine."

"You've helped us. If there's something we could do for you...?"

Her smile turned pained, but she shook her head. "I'll be okay."

I glanced at the guys. There wasn't anything for it. If she didn't want to talk or ask for help...

Asher seemed to come to the same conclusion. Coming up next to me, he nodded for me to follow Liam to the door. "Thank you," Asher told her as we paused on the porch. "And if you do ever need anything... just ask. We'll be there."

Her eyes flicked over to him, and after a heartbeat, her head twitched down in a single nod. "Thank you."

It might've been my imagination, but it felt like the trees were closing in at our backs as we walked, slowly erasing the trail to the cottage. Whatever was going on back there, the forest itself seemed to be protecting Eden from it.

I hated to leave her like this. It felt wrong, like abandoning a friend.

But maybe there'd be a chance to help her in the future.

Assuming we survived.

A quiver ran through me. The memory of burning alive was so fresh in my mind, making me want to rub my arms if only to be sure they were still whole. The day wasn't too bright, the afternoon sun barely making it past the thick foliage to leave the narrow track dappled with light while the forest around us was lost in deep shadows. But even that made me want to hide. I knew I had my protection from the sun again, thanks to Asher's and Ulysses' blood—and their compassion too. I wouldn't burn, not again. And while, yes, Urlfeige was still after us, we were safe right now.

I was safe.

Now if only I could convince my pounding heart of that.

Birdsong carried from somewhere overhead, far away and drowned beneath the rising tide of the past. We'd walked through forests like this so many times, traveling during the day to avoid Urlfeige's soldiers. It still hadn't been enough, though. He'd hunted us endlessly.

He still was.

A light touch brushed my arm, and I glanced over to see Asher watching me. "Are you okay?" he asked.

I nodded quickly.

His brow rose, silently questioning.

I shook my head, and he stepped closer, his hand taking mine. My body quivered, torn between now and far back then.

"We're okay," he whispered.

I made an agreeing noise, my eyes flashing between the two of them. They were Asher and Liam, Zerick and Seterios, and so much more than simple names could ever contain. And soon—God, please soon—we'd have the others back too.

My heart ached.

"Hey." Asher bent slightly to catch my eyes. "We're here now. Nothing that came before needs to matter as much as that, okay?"

I nodded. My hand lifted, brushing Asher's cheek. His eyes slipped closed, a look on his face as if he felt my touch all the way to his bones, no matter what he said about leaving the past in the past.

But I finally understood why I'd been so drawn to them all. Why I'd felt like I knew each of them, even when I hadn't. Why all of it. Why everything.

And now...

I reached out for Liam, and relief coursed through me when he took my hand. We were ourselves, not just past lives living out the same story again. We wouldn't be. But the ages apart still ached, and I couldn't take the pain any longer.

I stepped closer to Asher, my body tingling as if every nerve was coming alive, and I heard the soft sounds of Liam drawing nearer to me too. Their scents surrounded me—cold, crisp winter; woodsmoke and iron—and I breathed them in deep. Asher drew me to him, nipping at my lips like he was tasting me before his mouth claimed my own. Liam moved in behind me, his lips brushing along the curve between my shoulder and my neck, and his hands slid around my hips, pulling my ass to the length of hard cock beneath his pants.

"Yes," I whispered, breaking away from Asher briefly. "God, please, I need you both."

In a swift motion, Asher lifted me, and my legs wrapped around him, pulling my aching flesh tight against his cock. I ground on him, catching a glimpse of Liam slipping around us and leading the way from the trail into the forest, before I returned to kissing along Asher's jaw and neck. I could feel his pulse beating strongly against my lips, and the urge to bite down was overwhelming.

But I needed to wait until we were somewhere safer to taste him again.

In powerful strides, Asher's legs scaled the slope through the forest while I breathed in his scent and reveled in how every step rocked my clit against him. I was wet as hell, probably soaking my jeans as much as my underwear, and already I could feel the thrum of an orgasm building in my core.

It'd been hours since I'd had any of them. It'd been lifetimes.

Either was too long.

The air cooled and the light disappeared. I drew back, looking around to find that Liam had led us to a cave. Stripping off his jacket, he tossed it aside and then arched an eyebrow at Asher.

Lowering me from my perch around him, Asher regarded me with a hint of a wicked smile on his face. "Clothes off, Wren."

I hadn't thought I could get any more wet, but the delicious command in his voice made my pussy clench. At lightning speed, I shed my clothing while he and Liam did the same.

I started to sink toward the ground when a cautioning sound from Asher made me pause.

"I want to try something else." He stepped closer to me, his hard cock drawing my attention until his fingers took my chin, pulling my focus back up to his eyes. "I know you can do it." His other hand slipped between my legs, playing over my clit and nearly making my knees buckle. "But if at any point you want to stop, you only have to say it, understand?"

My head twitched in a nod.

His eyes flicked over to Liam, and his brow twitched up, a silent repetition of the offer to stop in his eyes.

Liam nodded, but he stepped nearer too, his hands ghosting over my hips and then around to my ass.

Asher's wicked smile returned. Quickly, he hefted me up, but he held me above his cock, not entering me yet.

I whimpered, writhing a little in protest, wanting him in me right now. And then Liam's fingers slipped into me. My eyes went wide as he began stroking me from within, and in only moments, my nascent orgasm overtook me. I cried out as my pussy clenched around him, and my body rocked as I rode out the waves of pleasure.

"Good girl," Asher whispered.

God, I could feel my desire slickening his abs, I was so turned on.

Liam withdrew from inside me, and I restrained a whimper, craving one of them filling me again. I threw a look over my shoulder to see him coating his cock with my slick, and my lips parted at what I thought he might be preparing to do.

"Focus, gorgeous," Asher said.

I looked back at him just in time for him to pull me down onto his cock. I gasped, trying to rock on him immediately.

He made a cautioning noise, holding me still. "We're not done yet."

Liam's fingers returned, sliding and massaging at my other opening. I moaned, my core turning molten as pleasure radiated out from the nerves he was stimulating. After a moment, one of his fingers penetrated me, and I tried to push against him, wanting more.

Asher chuckled. "Greedy."

More of Liam's fingers slid in, prepping me and driving me wild, only to disappear.

And be replaced by his cock.

I gasped as he started inside me, my eyes squeezing shut at the burn and yet the pleasure of my body stretching to take him in. But soon, the burn faded, overwhelmed by the sheer ecstasy of both of them filling me.

And then they began moving.

I moaned, my eyes going wide at the pleasure growing stronger with their every thrust. Soon, I couldn't even recognize the sounds coming from me. Pleading noises, begging them never to stop, never to even *think* about stopping. Asher held my hips, controlling my rocking against him, while Liam's fingers stole up to roll and pinch my nipple, making me whimper and writhe between them. I was theirs and they were mine, and my whole body thrummed with the sensations of them driving into me, their enormous cocks penetrating me so deeply, I saw stars.

This was it. What I needed. My men filling me, taking pleasure with me. This was everything.

"That's it," Asher murmured to me. "Just like that. Our warrior princess."

I started to smile, but just at that moment, Liam's free hand slipped down, flicking over my clit. I gasped, my orgasm taking me so fast, stealing everything in a wave of pure ecstasy as I cried out their names in the darkness of the cave. But neither of the men stopped, only thrusting into me harder and harder as sweat built between us and their delicious scents filled the air.

I was grateful they were holding me up. No way my legs would be more than jelly at this point.

Still, they kept going, their movements turning ragged

even as they kept thrusting hard, pinching and nipping at me, building me toward another orgasm.

But I wanted more now.

"Drink from me," I gasped at them. "Oh, God, please. Please, bite—"

Like cobras, they struck, one on each side of my throat, and I screamed as I came hard. The cave disappeared. White light and stars exploded behind my closed eyes. I was nothing but ecstasy and energy and the sensation of them taking in my blood, their thrusts turning savage as their orgasms overcame them too.

I sagged while they released my throat and licked the wounds closed quickly. My head dropped down to rest on Asher's shoulder. I felt limp after the orgasms they'd wrung from my body, and as Liam drew out of me and Asher turned, I could barely summon the energy to wonder what they were doing now.

Something rustled and a few moments passed, and then Asher shifted me around. Liam's hands slipped around me, hefting me from Asher's arms.

I looked up, confused. Liam was dressed now, and as Asher moved to collect his own clothes, Liam sank down onto a shelf of stone by the wall. Gently, he held me on his lap, keeping me from the grit and dirt.

My heart stuttered in my chest. At my startled look, however, he just gave me a soft smile. "I can touch *you*," he whispered.

His arms tightened around me, and cautiously, I rested my head against his chest.

After a moment, Asher returned. He draped his jacket

over me and then sank down nearby. His fingers brushed back a strand of my hair from my face, and he smiled.

"I'll never get enough of you," he murmured.

I smiled, nestling against Liam and reveling in having them both here. "Likewise."

22

ASHER

Nearly a thousand years of this life, and I'd never felt like I did right now.

Not since my last lifetime with her.

Wren's eyes drifted shut as she rested against Liam's chest, and I smiled, happy for him that he could hold her. Happy she trusted us enough for us both to have her like we did, drink her like we had as she came around us.

Happy to have our Wren, our Tauluria, our beautiful woman back again.

I leaned against the stone wall of the cave. I couldn't begin to wrap my head around what had happened at Eden's house. I'd seen so many things over the nine hundred years I'd been Asher, but reincarnation? That was new. It did fill in some blanks—the true origin of our resistance to the sun, why I felt so drawn to Wren now. Hell, it even explained our knives. In that life, Tau had poured whatever power she could into them, lending strength to the runes and spells already carved into their surfaces, until their essence and ours joined. But Amalie must have been suppressing so much of our pasts and hers alike that they never appeared for us. Not until she was gone.

I sighed. I felt the same and yet different now, a contradiction of halves that were both the whole while remaining distinct. I had Zerick's memories. I could feel what it had been like to be him, and on some level, it was as familiar to me as my own skin.

But I was also still myself. Still Asher. It was as if someone had opened a hatchway in the floor of my life, and beneath lay a whole other world that had always been there; I'd just never known.

Yet... I'd felt its effects. I simply hadn't known what they meant.

Now I had my answer.

Wren's fingertips brushed my skin, tracing a gentle path up and down my forearm. I exhaled, relishing the feeling of her. It wasn't just her touch, though. I could feel *her*. Like the other Sentinels, yet even stronger than that. I'd been more right than I knew when I felt like she connected us all.

She sighed, and I refocused on her. She was watching the cave entrance, regret on her face, and I had a suspicion as to why. Sunset was coming. Already, I could see how it was lengthening the shadows beyond the entrance. The cave around us was nearly dark, and the shadows would've been impenetrable if not for our night vision. Soon enough, the rabids would be able to come outside again and nowhere would be safe. We needed to leave as soon as we could.

And go somewhere with a real bed, and some privacy too.

Wren raised an eyebrow at me. "You're smiling. What is it?"

I shrugged. "Just thinking about doing this again, maybe somewhere more comfortable."

She grinned. As he held her close, a dark smile full of anticipation crossed Liam's face.

Her eyes moved beyond me, though, landing on the cave entrance again, and her grin faded. "You think we can still save the others?"

The need to take away the pain I could hear in her voice had me pulling her to me. Liam helped shift her off his lap and into mine as my lips nipped at hers, trying to draw her focus back to better things. I didn't know whether we could save Ulysses or Gideon. Without help from Eden, our chances weren't good.

But I didn't want Wren to hurt over that reality right now.

Her lips parted, and swiftly, I deepened the kiss as I held her to me. She groaned deliciously against my lips, wiggling her beautiful ass on my lap. My cock hardened all over again, more than ready. The urge to plunge myself into her—or perhaps feel her pretty mouth around my length this time—was overwhelming.

But then, every passing minute brought us closer to sunset.

I made myself stop. Pulling away, I gave her a smile, and my heart tripped over itself at the way she looked at me with such trust.

She'd looked at me that way so long ago too.

My hands tightened on her. Those damn memories were determined to destroy this moment—or maybe just to make sure I *never* let anything like that happen again. I'd worried about watching her die, back before I recalled who we'd been millennia ago. But now that I actually remembered *seeing* that?

Gods below, I didn't care what I had to do. Nothing would steal her away from me, turning her to dust in my arms. Not ever again.

"Asher?" She put a hand to my cheek. "What is it?"

I shook my head, shoving the memories away. "Nothing."

Despite my smile, she didn't look entirely reassured, but she didn't press for more as I shifted around, lifting her to her feet as I rose. My cock ached as she bent down to collect her clothes, every inch of her naked but for the coat around her shoulders. It was all I could do not to take her hips and join Liam in making her ours again.

But we were losing time.

"I don't want to go back to the farmhouse," Wren said as she pulled her clothes into place. "If Eden can't help us with Ulysses and Gideon, we need to find someone else."

I hesitated. It was safer, having her stay there. The place was so out of the way, it might as well be on the moon.

She looked up at me. "Right?"

My mouth tightened. "Yeah, but I don't want you at risk either."

"We already had this argument."

"Doesn't change anything."

Shivers crawled over my skin as she looked away. In

reality, everything had changed. I could *feel* her body in my arms, turning to ash. I could remember the expression on her face when she died. The idea of seeing that again —*ever*—made fear grip my throat like a vise.

Near the entrance, Liam looked back at us, appearing tormented as well. Swiftly, he signed, *Without any magic to break the hold Urlfeige has on them or stop dormants from turning rabid, we're fucked. We should just get her out of here.*

Wren shifted her weight, her hand flexing like she was resisting the urge to summon the sword. "What'd he say?"

I grimaced. "Eden was our best hope. Without a spell from her..."

"Maybe we don't need a spell. If what Eden said was true about me, and I could figure out how to do it again, then—"

"No."

"Asher—"

"That *killed* you last time."

"But what if I could figure out how *not* to die, and bring Ulysses and Gideon back instead?"

"And if Urlfeige gets his hands on you?"

Irritation flashed over her face. "We have to do *something*. Ulysses is slaughtering people, and God knows what Gideon is being forced to do. We can't leave them like this, so if there is a chance I can bring them back..." Her head shook. "I have to try."

Cursing internally, I looked away. I wouldn't risk her. It wasn't an option. I just didn't have a plan to cover all our bases yet.

"So where to now?" Wren pressed, crouching to pull

on her shoes. "That video came from St. Louis, right? How do we find him there?"

Debating silently, I glanced at Liam.

Find a better solution, he signed at me while she wasn't looking, demand clear in every swift motion. *She is* not *dying again.*

I nodded.

Wren straightened. "Guys?"

Displeasure clear on his face, Liam looked away.

I scowled. "We need some place to get through the night first."

Her brow twitched down, but I didn't explain further. Checking carefully beyond the cave entrance and keeping her behind me, I headed into the forest again. Birds still darted between trees, and I could hear creatures moving in the underbrush, but nothing lunged out to attack us.

I didn't relax a bit.

By the time we made it back to the SUV, the sun was already sinking below the horizon, and all the long shadows from the trees had melted into one solid blanket of gray. Soon, rabids would be out hunting for her, for us, for anything they could sink their teeth into.

I floored the pedal and peeled away from the patch of gravel that probably had been a forest preserve parking spot before being abandoned years ago.

Now it just served as Eden's driveway, not that almost anyone else knew that.

When we reached the main road, the sky was sinking toward a shade of darker denim blue, and in short order, stars began to appear. Along the highway, farms were lit up in radioactive brilliance in the night.

Hours passed, and finally, we turned into the gravel parking lot of The Dirt Nap. The place looked more like a dump than any location where you would take your family. The weathered wooden walls were so splintered, it was amazing any nails still held them in place, and every slat had turned gray in the sun and rain. Windows crusted with grease and dust served to obscure the interior, turning the light inside into a murky glow, but neon signs for beer beamed their names out into the night.

I pulled the SUV to a stop and turned off the engine, scanning the few other vehicles dotting the lot. They could be decoys or they could belong to slayers for all I knew. Lazarus didn't discriminate. As long as you didn't start a fight—or at least could finish it without causing too much trouble—he didn't care who you were or what you did.

I glanced over at Wren. "Stay put, eh?"

She gave me an incredulous look. "Not likely."

"I don't know what's in there."

"Well, then we go together, and we find out."

I ground my teeth. She wasn't going to make this easy.

Like she ever had, even before this lifetime?

"You stay behind me. And if you see a slayer or rabid, you run. Deal?"

Stubbornness took up residence on her face. I arched an eyebrow at her.

"Fine," she said. "As long as you do too."

"Fine."

I cast a glance back at Liam and saw displeasure on his face, though whether it was for me or for her, I couldn't be sure.

Maybe both.

I pushed the door open and climbed out, eyeing the sky and the boundaries of the parking lot lights equally. Nothing jumped out at us, though that didn't mean rabids couldn't be rushing back to tell Amalie we were here.

Though, if that happened, I just had to hope Lazarus's defenses would help us, at least long enough to get away.

Clenching my fist against the urge to summon my knife, I headed for the door. The porch sagged under our feet as we climbed the steps. I was fairly certain that even though each bar Lazarus owned looked different from the others—at least in shape, if not, general anesthetic—he basically created them from the same spell box. The porch was always weathered. The windows were always grimy. Whether he actually sold any of those beers, I wasn't sure. The gods knew I never asked.

When we went inside, the main room of the bar appeared empty. Round tables dotted the space, while booths lined the left wall. The bar itself ran along the righthand side, stretching all the way to the back, ending in an exit door. Bottles gleamed on the wall, and behind the bar, Lazarus was drying a glass, never pausing even as he looked up to see who had walked in.

"Didn't expect to see you all." Despite his words, his face gave away no hint of surprise.

"We need a place to crash for the night."

"Gave you that. What'd you do to my farmhouse?"

"Nothing. We're handling the other problem."

He was quiet for a moment. "I take it you saw the video I sent of your guy."

I nodded.

His mouth tightened. "Bad business, that."

"Do you know where he is?"

"No more than you. Kid's somewhere in St. Louis—or he was." He paused. "Do you all have a plan for dealing with him?"

I hesitated, not taking my eyes from him and certainly not looking anywhere near Wren. "Something like that."

"Hmm."

He set down the glass and picked up another in a motion so smooth, it seemed automatic. The swish of the towel was the only sound.

"How bad is it out there?" Wren asked quietly.

Lazarus's eyes flicked over, and I resisted the urge to move protectively in front of her. Laz probably wasn't a threat. Maybe.

As much as an immortal older than me and Liam combined could be.

"Something's going down in St. Louis," he told her. "Not much word about it yet, but the GSS are there. In force. Consortium's got the under-city on lockdown too."

My teeth ground as I bit back a curse.

"They're staying under the radar right now. Local law enforcement's talking about an uptick in muggings or animal attacks, some murders, but the fact they're still talking at *all* tells me the GSS doesn't think the cops know enough for them to shut those folks up yet. But the slayers are still quietly cordoning off sections of town and setting up checkpoints to pick up on supernaturals in the area. Real hard to get into the city now without hitting one of them."

I blew out a breath. Fantastic. Of course the slayers

had seen that video too. Or heard chatter on the web about something vampire-related going on in St. Louis. Hell, their director, Lacrette, had even tried to make a deal with Amalie and Urlfeige.

Before they tore her to shreds.

And now they were surrounding the area where we'd probably find Ulysses.

"Any routes you know of?" I asked the immortal.

He shrugged. "I'll make some calls. See if I can find someone who has a way in. You all can crash upstairs in the meantime."

I paused. "Thanks."

My skepticism at the sheer amount of help he was offering had to be obvious.

He smiled and set down the glass he'd been drying. "I don't take sides, kid. Usually. But I remember Amalie's day. Legends of hard times before that too. And what they're playing at here..."

His eyes turned to the grimy windows, and suddenly, his gaze wasn't that of some indeterminately middle-aged man. It was that of someone who'd watched the Romans fall, and the Huns, and countless empires before them. Who'd seen more cities burn than I even knew names for.

I was old. But there was a reason Lazarus called us all *kid.*

He sighed. "Bad times are coming. I'd just as soon stay clear, but inaction is action too."

Wasn't that the truth. "You have any other folks here right now?" I nodded in the general direction of the parking lot and the cars outside.

He drew a breath, everything vanishing behind the

disinterested expression he usually wore. "Nah. Cars in the lot belong to a few shifters running through the woods. They won't be back till morning."

I glanced at the door. There was still the chance Amalie had gotten some shifters on the payroll.

But what option did we have? Lazarus's defenses were better than driving out in the open now that the sun had set.

"Don't suppose you want to introduce me to your friend?" Lazarus asked.

I tensed. He probably knew who she was already, but that didn't mean that I wanted to say it out loud.

There wasn't much choice. "Wren, meet Lazarus."

"Hi," Wren said warily.

He nodded at her and then took something from beneath the bar and tossed it to me.

Keys clinked in my hand when I caught them instinctively.

"Top of the stairs, right-side door," he said. "I'll let you know what I find out. And if y'all want to park whatever vehicle you drove back behind the bar, it'd probably be a good idea, just in case the slayers stop by. I have a tarp out back you could throw over it too."

I eyed him. "Sounds good."

He continued drying the glass.

I tossed Liam the keys to whatever rooms were upstairs. Catching them smoothly, he motioned for Wren to go with him toward the back while I headed for the front door. With one hand on the weathered wood, I paused. "Thanks, Laz. We owe you for this."

The man's lip twitched. "Hell yes, you do. Now get."

Shaking my head at it all, I went to move the SUV.

Everything outside looked just as we'd left it. The bright lights overhead, the few cars scattered around the parking lot, the dark forest beyond. I studied the trees, wondering if the shifters were out there and if they could see me. But I didn't feel any hint of rabids around me, and as I walked toward the SUV, my boots crunching on the gravel was the only sound.

Quickly, I climbed in and pulled around behind the bar. Courtesy of the blazing lights overhead, there wasn't a single shadowy spot where I could tuck it out of sight. But the tarp Lazarus had mentioned was lying on a stack of boxes by the back door, folded up and ready for my use.

The thing was probably magical. Most everything around here was. If you lived as long as Lazarus, you picked up more than a few tricks.

The hairs prickled on the back of my neck.

I didn't turn around, continuing to drape the plastic cloth over the SUV. If it was shifters, I'd hear them coming. Rabids, I'd feel.

And staring at the darkness would only keep them from attacking and getting this over with.

A low chuckle carried from behind me. I turned as a scruffy guy sauntered up to the edge of the parking lot.

Rabid.

On either side of him, four more vampires shifted from shadow to human form.

The first guy grinned. "Well, look at what we have here. The mistress is going to love this."

Fuck.

Three of them turned into shadows, racing at me, while the other two took off toward the door to the bar.

My knife was in my hand before they'd even finished shifting. I slashed at the shadows, but they twisted away, one of them trying to get behind me while the other went for my arm. My blade found the first rabid, and he fell back, shrieking with pain as the cut burned and chewed into his form.

A twist of shadow wrapped my throat. I flipped the knife in my hand and stabbed back at the rabid, but the creature evaded me as it squeezed down as if trying to take off my head. The third rabid charged at my chest, its shadowed form narrowing like a spear.

My body erupted into shadow and smoke.

Instinct sent me darting out of the way even as shock reverberated through me. The one rabid slammed into its ally, both creatures accidentally tearing into each other with their impact. Wounded and snarling with pain and rage, they whirled toward me.

A shotgun blast shattered the night, and my attention snapped to the side just in time to see one of the rabids who had been racing for the door suddenly burst into flame. Another blast took the next rabid only a moment later.

Lazarus leveled his gun at the rabids around me, but I could see the frustration on his face. In our shadow forms, he couldn't tell who was who.

The rabids lunged at me. The energy of my knife burned them alive as I slashed through them.

I shifted back as the creatures died behind me, and for a moment, I could only stare at my own arms and legs. How had I gained the power to shift again?

My eyes went to the second floor of the bar. In all the chaos of our lives, only one thing had recently changed.

Gods...

Lazarus muttered a curse as he turned back and went inside, and a moment later, a wave of magic rolled past me like electricity on the air. Along the edge of the gravel, the air flared bright, a vibrant blue-green shimmer racing around the lot and up over the bar like an enormous sphere of light. As quickly as it had appeared, the shimmer faded, leaving only a faint warping to my view of anything beyond the lot.

My brow rose. Clearly, Lazarus was furious if he was willing to risk putting up magic that a passerby might have seen.

I glanced at the forest. As before, I couldn't feel any rabids out there. But that might only mean they were far enough away that my senses couldn't detect them. Right now, they could be going to tell Amalie and Urlfeige where we were.

Dammit.

When I reached the main room of the bar again, Lazarus was already on the phone. "Yeah, well, I've got someone looking to get into St. Louis, so what do you have?" A heartbeat passed. "Hello? Hel— Oh, for fuck's sake." He scowled at the phone and then started dialing again.

Leaving him to it, I crossed the bar and climbed the stairs toward the second floor.

Liam opened the door while I was still halfway up the steps, his knife gripped in his hand.

"Rabids," I said. "Gone now."

He didn't look pleased. I didn't blame him.

When I reached the landing, I spotted Wren through the open doorway to my right. Her sword was in her hand as well, the gleaming white blade more light than form and throwing off sparks that hinted at how tense she must be. The sight of her gripping the hilt stole my breath, more memories from my past life rushing up to make me swear yet again that nothing would ever hurt her.

Not while I still walked the earth.

Ordering myself to focus, I continued through the door. The room around her looked like it belonged in a run-down motel. A cheap plastic light fixture hung over a chipped Formica table to the left. A kitchen nook waited beyond it, though it was barely more than a sink, a single plywood cupboard pinned to the wall, and an electric hot plate serving as the stove on the scuffed countertop beneath it. On the opposite side of the room, the mattress was covered in a blanket that somehow defied my eyes to decide whether it was blue or gray. All around, the walls were a drab sort of white that edged toward gray too, and I couldn't see a window anywhere.

Which was good for security but must have left both Liam and Wren wondering what the hell was going on outside.

"I thought I heard gunshots," Wren said as if proving my thoughts.

"Lazarus. He shot the few that made a break for the door. He's upped the defenses around this place now, too."

Liam's eyes narrowed at me. *Then what's wrong?*

I hesitated. "I can shift again."

His brow climbed.

"But I thought—" Wren started.

Liam shifted into shadow and smoke, hovering for only a moment before reverting. "How?" he demanded roughly the moment he was back in human form.

I glanced at Wren.

She blinked. "*I* didn't—"

"What else is there?"

"Coincidence?"

I doubted it.

The connection is stronger, Liam signed. *A* lot *stronger.*

"Between you four?" Wren asked.

I shook my head. "To you."

Her mouth moved, but it took a moment for any sound to emerge. "Well... what's that mean?"

I met her eyes, certainty settling in me. "That maybe you were right. There might be a way you can save them."

23

WREN

I should have been elated by Asher's words. I *would* have been.

Except for one little thing.

"B-but I don't know what I did," I stammered. "Maybe I didn't do anything. What if whatever Urlfeige did just wore off or something?"

"Could we test it?" Asher asked, nodding toward the bed.

I blinked. "Um, I'm not sure sex is going to—"

"No." He winced as if embarrassed. "Just come here, please?"

I crossed the room to him, casting a glance back at Liam as I did.

Watching Asher, he made a cautioning noise, and I couldn't catch everything he signed.

"I'm not gambling with her," Asher countered. "We'll be here. But if this works, then we won't even need to go to St. Louis."

Shaking his head, Liam started to sign something else, and irritation flashed over Asher's face. "Hey, you *asked* for a better plan."

Liam's mouth tightened, but he didn't continue arguing.

"What are we testing?" I asked as I sank cautiously onto the side of the bed.

Asher sat down next to me. "Using the connection with you to reach them from here."

I blinked. "You said *you* couldn't even feel that link to them anymore. What makes you think I could?"

"The fact you might've just done something that even witches thought was impossible."

I stared at him.

"He's right," Liam said.

Asher tossed him a grateful look before returning his attention to me. "Better here where we're at a safe distance than closer where anything could happen."

I floundered. They really believed this. That somehow I had done this, even if I didn't know how. Or maybe that Tau had.

But I *was* her. I remembered her life, at least mostly. And I remembered how it had felt when I first realized I was connected with all of them, all those millennia ago. The impossible link had become like second nature to me in that lifetime, even if I'd never really understood it in this one.

An ache throbbed through me, distant but so painful. I'd wanted it back so badly, though. I hadn't even realized how much until now.

"Please, Wren," Asher said softly. "If this could give us an advantage, now is the time to find out."

"But what if Amalie could feel this somehow?"

"Then we get the hell out of here, and we find another way."

That didn't answer what she would do if she attacked me psychically.

But then, if she could do that, why hadn't she done it already?

I exhaled. "Okay. What do we do?"

Asher's relief was palpable. He reached out, taking my hand.

"Close your eyes," he said. "Feel inside of yourself for a sense of connection to me."

My brow furrowed slightly. Whenever I picked up on it in this lifetime, the connection they talked about had just been an amorphous sense, as unpredictable as a cloud formation, passing through me like a tickle in my mind that made no sense. But it wasn't something I could *find*. It just happened, all on its own. Even as Tau, when I knew what the hell I was feeling, I'd never had to search for it.

It simply was.

"Try, Wren," Asher urged, watching me. "Please."

Nodding, I closed my eyes.

Moments passed, ticking away, and nothing happened. Was I doing something wrong?

"It's not working," I said.

"Think about how you summon the sword," Asher replied. "Like that, but... different."

Oh, *that* wasn't vague.

Exhaling sharply, I attempted to make myself do as he said, but the frustration was hard to get over. If I couldn't even do *this*, how was I going to help Ulysses or Gideon?

My eyes squeezed shut tighter. I needed this to work. *They* did. I couldn't let them down—or Asher and Liam for that matter.

An amorphous sense of Asher surfaced in my mind.

My breath caught. He was there, in me. *Part* of me, but like a tinge of color to the sky or sudden warmth on the breeze. How the hell I knew it was him, I could barely define. It was just... his energy. His warmth. His heart. Everything I knew as Asher, and so much more. And there, too, was Liam like a cool and gentle breeze and a savage winter wind, but one that would never harm me, only protect. They were both simultaneously around me, with me, not canceling each other out but somehow just bringing more depth to the world.

Was this what it felt like for them too? The sense that no matter which way I reached out my hand, they would be there?

It was wonderful.

A smile pulled at my lips. I could feel the care and compassion from them. The comfort. My eyes flew open, and I lost the clarity of my awareness of them, but not the sense that they were still there, constantly with me.

All I could do was stare at them.

Asher's brow twitched up. "I take it that might've worked?"

I nodded, not sure what to even say.

"Can you feel that for either of the others?" he asked me.

I bit my lip and closed my eyes again, concentrating. I couldn't believe I'd missed picking up on them until now.

But I still didn't feel quite right, as if part of my body was missing. Part of the color in the world, too, leaving some of reality unsaturated. Not black or white or gray, but just... void. An emptiness where color should have been, making life less vivid with its absence.

Except, on second thought...

My brow furrowed as I concentrated harder. At the edge of my mind, in the darkness of the horizon, there was a tinge of color. Just a hint, so far away from me that at any moment felt like it was going to disappear.

Out of nowhere, panic gripped me. I couldn't let it vanish. If it went away, it'd be gone forever. Not just from me, but from everything.

From itself.

I strained toward it, reaching in my mind, desperate to get to it before it fell into the abyss entirely. But no matter how hard I tried, it never came closer, as if gravity was pulling that beautiful, rich tinge of color away from me, keeping it forever at a distance.

Desperation built inside of me like a pressure, driving me onward. I couldn't lose this, not again. I'd been separated from them before, and I hadn't even known it. I couldn't go back to that, not now that I could feel them again.

I stretched farther, the strain tearing at me. It was there. One of the bright colors in my universe, and if I could just... just...

"Wren!"

My eyes flew open, jarring me back to reality. Asher

was crouched in front of me, gripping my shoulders. Nearby, Liam was watching me with alarm.

Asher had been shaking me, I realized. I felt light-headed, as if I'd been hyperventilating, and on my face, I could feel moisture.

I reached up and then blinked as I drew my hand back. Red blood mixed with tears on my fingertips.

Liam vanished into the bathroom swiftly, returning a moment later with a towel. Worry in his eyes, he pressed it gently to my nose to stop the bleeding.

"What..." My voice was muffled by the towel.

"Was it Amalie?" Asher asked, not letting go of me.

I started to shake my head and then stopped when it felt like my brain sloshed against my skull. "Gideon."

His name just came to me, like somehow that distant presence on the horizon of my mind could only be him.

"*He* did this?" Asher sounded furious.

"No. No, just..." I took the towel from Liam and tilted my head back, hoping the bleeding would stop. "I wanted to reach him, but something was keeping him away from me." My eyes stung all over again. Squeezing them shut briefly, I fought not to cry.

Asher shifted around, sitting on the bed and putting an arm around my shoulders. "What about Ulysses?"

Grief pressed down on me like part of my own heart had been ripped away. "I couldn't... If he was there, I couldn't feel him."

Liam sank down on my other side. I sat between them, the connection we shared surrounding and comforting me.

The feeling was surreal, like finding a home I'd

forgotten I had. And more than that, even. Because while I remembered how Tau felt about it, I also knew how *I* felt. A few weeks ago, I'd been a college student studying history, no dating prospects on the horizon and not particularly interested in finding them either. And then life had gone utterly mad, but it had delivered these men to me, unasked and unexpected.

I couldn't imagine going back to a world without them.

We *had* to find the others. Even if Gideon didn't care for me, even if he wanted nothing to do with me, it didn't matter. I still wanted him safe, no matter what. And as for Ulysses...

That pain lodged in my chest again, aching. I didn't want to think about whether we had lost him. It felt unfathomable.

At a soft sound from Liam, I looked over.

Could you tell where Gideon was? he signed.

I thought back. "South. About a hundred miles?"

"St. Louis?" Asher asked.

"Maybe?"

Asher turned away, his jaw tightening.

"I'm not staying here," I said immediately.

His eyes were tinged with frustration when he looked back at me, but he didn't argue.

Liam took my hand. His touch always felt like a precious gift, even now. It was still a sign of closeness that I was fairly certain he didn't share with many people. Maybe no one at all.

"So what's the plan?" I asked.

Both men were silent.

"I could feel Gideon out there. And if we were closer, maybe I could find Ulysses too." A quiver rolled through me. "Maybe I could bring him back."

Asher closed his eyes, his brow furrowing. "Okay. We'll see if Lazarus can find us a way to at least get closer to wherever they have Gideon and Ulysses."

Liam frowned. *And Ulysses' knife?* he asked, his expression making clear he wasn't sold on this idea. *Won't help us if we free him only to have Amalie take control again.*

"Maybe he or Gideon will know where it is," I said.

He looked away.

I squeezed his hand. I knew this was a long shot made up of maybes, but we couldn't leave them. And worst of all, I was fairly sure Amalie knew that.

Which meant she might be waiting for us.

A knock came at the door. Kissing my forehead briefly, Asher got up. His knife appeared in his grip while he crossed the room, and I could feel Liam's tension in how tightly he gripped my hand.

But it was only Lazarus on the other side. He scanned us all with a flat look that I couldn't hope to read and then said, "I got you a way in."

24

LIAM

I was Liam and I was Seterios, and as I followed Lazarus downstairs with the others, all *either* part of me wanted to do was take Wren in my arms again and get the hell away from anything that could threaten her.

Even if I knew she'd never go. Our fierce warrior princess. Gods help us, she never backed down.

No matter what.

My eyes flicked around the bar's empty main room. As before, the space was still, every chair still tucked under the rough wooden tables and the jukebox in the corner utterly silent.

I still didn't trust it. The protectiveness I'd felt toward Wren before had just amplified a thousandfold, thanks to the horrific memory of watching her die in Zerick's arms. The pain of that moment was etched on my soul. *Nothing* would touch her.

Not if it wanted to stay on this side of death.

"So what'd you find?" Asher asked Lazarus.

"Well…" The man exhaled, continuing around behind the bar. "They're going to meet you at their place of business. One of them, anyway."

My instincts went on high alert. That wasn't what Asher had asked, and I could tell that the immortal barkeeper knew it.

Who? I demanded.

"We needed a route, not people, Laz," Asher added.

Lazarus hesitated, and a sinking feeling took up residence in my stomach. This wouldn't be good. "It's a bit more complicated than that," he admitted.

Asher glanced at me briefly. "How?"

"Well, rumor has it your girl's the one everybody's after."

I tensed, ready to summon my knife in an instant if he looked like a threat to Wren—immortal or not.

"Stories out there are getting pretty wild. Saying anyone she lays eyes on turns into a rabid, that sort of thing." He tilted his head at Wren. "Obviously, that's not true, seeing as you're looking right at me, and I don't have the least inclination for blood."

None of us said a word.

"But the Consortium has put out a damn big bounty on her. You lot too, by extension. I had to fend off more than a few folks who took my questions as info that you all were here and ripe for the picking."

Fuck.

"Got you a way in, though."

Asher's expression was grim. "Who?"

He paused. "Cerberus."

"No," Asher said immediately.

Are you crazy? I signed at the man.

"They're the only ones who would agree to help."

Wren looked between all of us. "Who is Cerberus?"

"Not an option," Asher answered.

Lazarus made an irritated noise. "You needed a way in. I found you a way in."

"I didn't think you'd go with the *psychopaths*."

"Wait, what?" Wren protested, incredulous.

Wolf shifters, I explained.

"Three *insane* wolf shifters." Asher looked back at Lazarus. "How the hell were they the best option?"

"If you have another offer on the table, go for it." Lazarus offered us an old cordless phone. "Cerberus hates the Consortium, and you know it. But the bureaucrats have Gateway on lockdown while the vampires and GSS are roaming aboveground, and damn near everybody wants a piece of her." He jerked his head at Wren. "Who else are you going to find?"

Wren's attention snapped toward Lazarus. "Wait, Gateway? Like Gateway City?"

He gave a short nod, not taking his attention from Asher. "Every contact I have in St. Louis and Gateway either wants the bounty or wants nothing to do with vampires at all—Sentinels included. Everyone's got their own theory on why your lot are in St. Louis, but they all know something big is brewing. There aren't enough favors or bribes in the world to get folks involved with a fight between your kind right now."

"Except for *Cerberus*," Asher retorted.

Lazarus scoffed. "Nobody else crazy enough."

I shook my head. *We need a better option.*

"There *isn't* one," Lazarus countered.

Wren looked between us all. "If they're so crazy, why did they agree to help us?"

Lazarus' brow shrugged. "Let's just say they have a problem with authority—doesn't matter what kind." He paused. "And they want to make a deal with you all."

"*Hell* no," Asher snapped.

"Come on, kid," Lazarus scoffed. "How else are you going to get in there to help your boys? If anyone is going to have a route past the GSS, the Consortium, *and* the vampires, you know it's going to be those three crazy fucks."

I scowled.

"And when they try to sell us out?" Asher retorted.

"*If* they do..." Lazarus shrugged. "Kill them. The Consortium's wanted Cerberus dead for years. The bureaucrats will owe you, and maybe you can use that as a bargaining chip to keep their hands off your girl."

My teeth ground as Asher gave me a brief glance, and I could read the look on his face. I hated this. So did he. But most of all, we hated that Lazarus was right. If there was a bounty on Wren—and on us too—then just driving into St. Louis was a fast track to getting captured by the first opportunistic supernatural who spotted us.

And every other contact we had was a risk, now more than ever.

"Fine." Asher scrubbed a hand across his head. "Cerberus it is."

25

WREN

The ride in the SUV was silent after we left Lazarus's bar. Liam and Asher had both sunk into their own private worlds, and from their expressions, I suspected they were envisioning all the numerous ways this could go wrong. And I didn't know what to offer them. There was a *bounty* on our heads. Were there wanted posters out there too, like this was the Wild West or something?

Some part of me just wanted to laugh, though nothing about this was funny. We were being hunted, and so we were traveling to see three apparent psychopaths who were going to sneak us into St. Louis like fugitives.

How the hell was this my life?

I slouched lower in the back seat, trying to stay out of sight behind the smoked windows. To hear Lazarus talk, it sounded like St. Louis was under siege by the vampires and the GSS—not that any regular humans seemed to know it.

And underneath it all was Gateway City, whatever that was.

God, I hoped Ollie, Emma, and Brayden were okay—aboveground or below.

After about an hour, we came to an intersection at the end of the narrow road we'd been following across the countryside. A green road sign directly in front of us showed arrows pointing in one direction toward the highway and in the other toward the small town that was our destination.

The SUV came to a stop and didn't go any farther.

I glanced at Asher. His hands flexed on the steering wheel, and he eyed the sign ahead of us like it was personally responsible for this mess.

"Can you think of a better option?" I asked quietly.

He scowled, but after a moment, he pressed the pedal down again and turned the SUV toward the town.

I sighed. The farmland around us was a dark abyss. There was no moonlight, no stars. The overcast sky was a sheet of black, and beneath it, I couldn't even see a billboard glowing in the dark.

It'd be so easy for rabids to come up on us unawares, part of me wondered if we shouldn't have waited until sunrise.

But then, every minute that ticked away only left Gideon and Ulysses with Amalie longer.

The road curved around a line of trees tracing a river, and the lights of a small town came into view ahead. In the back seat, I trembled, watching the place as we drove closer. It looked... peaceful. A local gas station here, a family restaurant closed for the night there. They even had a drive-in movie theater just outside town, though I'd never seen one in real life so it took me a minute to realize what it even was. But after the destruction of my hometown and three weeks hiding out in a crumbling farmhouse in the middle of nowhere, the utter *normalcy* felt surreal.

Asher steered the SUV through the streets, and my eyes skirted away from the people inside the gas station and outside a local bar, just in case I might be a danger to them. "Do you know if there are any dormants here?" I murmured.

Liam glanced back at me, signing briefly. *Not sure.*

Great.

I was a ball of tension hiding in the back seat by the time Asher turned onto a road lined with brick buildings without windows on their sides. Old warehouses or factories, maybe, each backing up on the railroad track I could see in the spaces between them. After a few more yards, Asher pulled the SUV over and brought it to a stop, his eyes on something ahead.

"That one," he said, jerking his chin toward a building half a block down on the opposite side of the road.

Weathered paint on the sides marked the building as some kind of clothing company, though the name was so chipped and faded, I couldn't read the letters. It was anyone's guess if that was still what existed within those walls. Given who we were meeting, I doubted it.

"Limited exits," Liam said in a low voice behind me. "Few windows. Heavily defensible."

"They'll have other ways out," Asher said. "We just won't know what they are."

"So..." I fidgeted and then stopped myself. "Trap?"

"A box that will be hard to escape, at least." Asher glanced over at me, and I braced myself, ready to protest yet again that he wasn't leaving me here.

But he didn't say that. "Just stay behind me."

I nodded.

His eyes flicked back to Liam, some kind of unspoken understanding seeming to pass between them. And then he turned and pushed open the door.

The night was still as we left the SUV behind. Even the breeze was gone, and in a town like this, there weren't any streetlights nearby to beat back the dark. For the first time, I found myself wishing that my body wasn't emulating life. My heart and breathing felt too loud, as if a predator out in the darkness would pick up on it and come to get me.

We crossed the road and veered toward the side of the building. A door halfway along the brick length opened before we reached it, and two large men with guns in their hands stepped out.

Asher and Liam had me behind them before I could even register that they'd moved. But the men made no attempt to attack us, standing in silence beside the open door. They were enormous, built like the world had been running a surplus on muscles when they were created. The one on the left was slightly taller than the one on the right, though both would tower over me if I came close.

But their eyes marked them as something other than human, both pairs reflecting a sheen that reminded me of a wild animal in the darkness. An indefinable air of menace radiated from them, reinforcing the impression.

The two men looked us over briefly, and then the taller one nodded his bald head toward the open door. Asher's jaw muscles jumped, and ahead of me, Liam felt like a live wire. My hand itched to grab for my sword, but I knew that wouldn't go well. In silence, we walked to the door and past the big guys, Asher staying in the lead while Liam fell back to keep himself between me and the strangers.

Beyond the doorway, the space defied even my night vision to find any details, but as we walked inside, the closeness of the air made me feel like we were in a small space. The two men followed us in, shutting the door at our backs and sealing out the world.

Anxiety prickled along my spine. I'd been trapped in darkness like this before, after rabids kidnapped me and tried to drive me mad, if only to let Amalie take control. I'd been stuck in that cramped, pitch-black hell for days before they finally turned on a light.

The confines had felt like a grave.

Cold sweat broke out across my skin. I couldn't stop my breathing from picking up, coming in short, hard gasps. I *wasn't* back there again. I knew that, rationally, but repeating it to myself wasn't doing a damn thing to stop the sudden tide of panic rising in my head, threatening to drown me.

Liam's hand found the small of my back, rubbing small circles there while a wave of understanding and compassion swept over me through our bond. It felt like a safety net in the dark, stopping my fall. Like a cool, soft place to land.

My breathing slowed, the panic ebbing and gratitude

taking its place, though I didn't dare say a word with potential enemies nearby.

Somehow, I suspected Liam knew anyway.

One of the big guys slipped past us, moving more silently than it seemed like he should have, considering he'd towered over me and looked like he could bench-press a car. A small sound followed when he reached the opposite end of the space, almost like a switch flipping. For another moment, he waited, and then light stung my eyes when he pulled open a door.

I blinked, trying to get my vision to adjust.

It really *was* a clothing factory.

Bolts of cloth hung from the wall to my left, and the room was filled with row upon row of steel tables with industrial-looking sewing machines on top. Lights on metal arms were clamped to the side of each table, glaring down on the metal surface and making me wince at their brightness. The ceiling overhead wasn't any higher than a normal office building, but it was utilitarian in its tangle of lights, pipes, and wires. Only this room seemed to be lit, though. Between the bolts of cloth on the wall, hallways led off into darkness.

But we weren't alone.

I tensed, my attention fastening on the sinister shapes moving in the shadows. Eyes glimmered with a yellow-green sheen, changing to a human appearance as they stepped into the light. The men they belonged to looked like the type you'd cross the road to avoid—all leather and cold gazes that tracked every step we took. One had tattoos down the side of his face; another held a gun in his clasped hands so calmly it might as well have been part of him. Still another was so huge, I was amazed he'd been hidden by the shadows at all, his body towering nearly to the ceiling.

Clenching my fist to keep the sword from appearing and getting us killed, I stuck close to Asher and Liam while we crossed the long room toward a simple wooden door. The big guy leading us knocked once and then waited, the seconds ticking past with no change.

"Enter," came a deep voice from the other side.

The man clasped the brass handle, his large hand dwarfing the metal, and then pushed the door open.

In spite of myself, I swallowed hard at the sight of the three figures within. I wasn't sure what I'd expected, but this...

I wasn't even sure what *this* was.

A man who looked like a Fortune 500 CEO was seated to the left. He wore a dark suit and before him was a massive carved oak desk with only a single sheet of paper placed precisely in the center of the leather top. Leaning back in his chair with his hands folded in front of him, the calmness of his posture would have made an idiot let down their guard, but you only had to meet his eyes to know it'd be the last mistake you'd ever make.

The darkness there was chilling. Terrifying. I couldn't imagine a soul on earth would matter to him beyond what advantage they could bring. Without a trace of expression, he regarded us like he'd already run every angle of our upcoming conversation through his head, and now it was up to us to make sure we chose the correct things to say— the ones that kept us alive.

On the right, another man leaned against the wall, his

arms crossed in front of him and a knife the size of a machete clasped in one hand. He had to be nearly seven feet tall, wearing a dark t-shirt that clung to his inordinate amount of muscles, but nothing hinted that his size would make him slow. No, everything about him radiated *killer* like the word was painted in neon letters in the air. A savage scar crossed his face from the right side of his forehead all the way to his left jaw, and there wasn't a trace of emotion in his expression. As much as the large blade in his grip, he looked like a weapon quietly waiting for the order to strike.

But it was the guy in the middle who made me want to spin around and leave—except turning my back to him felt like a suicidal mistake. Sure, he held no weapons, and I couldn't see any scars on his lean body. Casually seated on the long couch directly opposite the door, one leg propped on the knee of the other and his arms stretched out on either side, he simply looked like some guy hanging out in a weird kind of office.

Except for how he was grinning, anyway. That smile said a guillotine was about to fall on our necks, and he was looking forward to the entertainment. His eyes glinted with gleeful madness, not a trace of sanity to be seen, while everything about him radiated anticipation, as if the whole world crumbling into chaos would be *entirely* his kind of party.

And he couldn't wait.

The CEO guy twitched his chin at the two men who'd brought us here. Without a word, they left.

I fought not to flinch as the door shut behind us, sealing us inside.

"You wished to speak with us?" the CEO said.

"Lazarus explained what we needed," Asher said.

The man nodded once. "Passage into and out of St. Louis undetected by the vampires, the Consortium, and the GSS. Tricky proposition, especially these days."

"He said you claimed you could do it."

The man smiled, nothing more than a flex of the muscles around his lips that didn't come close to touching his dark eyes. "We also explained there'd be a price."

Asher was silent for a moment. "And that is?"

"You have a number of properties scattered around the world, most of them with lengthy records of sale disguising that you're the owners. Right now, none of them are safe for you, and we understand that. However, we are interested in the home in North Umbria. You sign that over to us." He pushed the paper on his desk forward. "And when this is over, we claim it—whether or not you survive."

Asher stared at him. "You want a house?"

"And the surrounding structures that accompany the property, yes."

"Why?"

The man's eyebrow arched. "Is that relevant? This is our price. If you wish safe passage to and from St. Louis, you'll pay it."

Asher glanced at Liam for a moment. "Done," he said to the man behind the desk.

The crazy guy on the couch chuckled like a trap had snapped shut. My skin crawled.

"Very well, then." The man behind the desk rose to his feet and gestured to the paper in front of him. When

Asher approached, he withdrew a fountain pen from his suit jacket and extended it.

He smiled when Asher finished signing. "Now that that's concluded, I'm Silas. This is Gunnar." He nodded to the large man by the far wall. "And that is Axel." The guy on the couch didn't stop grinning like a maniac. "Let's deliver you to St. Louis, shall we?"

26

ASHER

Nothing about this was a good idea.

In eerie unison, the triumvirate known as Cerberus moved toward the door, and I shifted position quickly to prevent any of them from getting behind our backs. Every one of those three was a killer—ruthless, efficient, following no moral code but their own—but Axel especially had a reputation for being nothing short of an absolute psychopath. The stories I'd heard about that guy...

If we'd had any other option, I wouldn't have come within a hundred miles of him.

Silas gave us that cool smile again, like we'd been diced up and he was calculating the profit he'd get from selling our pieces.

Hundred miles of *any* of them.

Out on the factory floor, the group I'd seen earlier had evaporated as if they'd never existed. I spotted the security cameras perched almost invisibly in corners, though. Chances were, we were still being watched.

"This way," Silas said, gesturing to one of the halls to our right.

"After you," I replied.

Amusement tinged his smile. He shared a brief look with his companions and then turned, walking down the hallway. The massive wolf, Gunnar, followed while Axel grinned at us like a demented clown.

Make that a thousand miles. Could we take them? Probably. Did I want to start a war with the wolf shifter underground?

We had enough problems.

I heard Wren draw in air when Axel finally turned and followed the others, as if she had been holding her breath for the moment it took him to decide not to attack. I touched her arm, trying to let her know we were with her.

She gave me a tiny smile and drew another breath as if to steady herself.

At the end of the hall, the wolves came to a stop at a metal door with an unlit exit sign hanging above it. Briefly, Silas drew out his cell phone, checking something on the screen before tucking it away again. "Roads will be clear in ten minutes."

Gunnar nodded while Axel kept grinning. Without another word, Silas pushed open the door. A delivery bay with massive garage doors lay beyond the exit. Most of the lights were off, casting the place in deep shadow, but a few handheld utility lights glowed where they'd been scattered around the concrete floor, throwing the vehicles parked there into stark relief.

My brow twitched up as Silas and the others headed for an ambulance. It looked brand new, painted like it belonged to a local St. Louis hospital. But that wasn't what made my footsteps slow.

Garlic reeked from the thing, and there was a sheen to the sides like it was lightly crusted with salt.

Axel gave us a crazed grin. "Dried holy water and garlic extract." He made a sizzling sound.

Asshole.

"There's none of that on the inside." Silas twitched his chin to Gunnar, who tugged open the rear doors of the ambulance and then climbed inside. "Just avoid touching anything until you're in there."

I eyed the interior skeptically. "We're just going to hide in there and hope no one opens the door?"

I couldn't keep the dry note from my voice. As strategies went, this was about on par with putting on a pair of glasses and hoping no one recognized you.

Gunnar gave me a withering look. Turning, he pulled aside a panel in the floor. I walked closer, peering past the metal and trying to ignore the way it made my skin crawl.

A compartment lay below the floor of the ambulance. Cramped quarters, but possibly large enough for people to hide inside.

"In you go," Silas said.

I looked from the opening to the shifter. "Smuggle a lot of people in here, do you?"

He gave me an enigmatic smile that could have meant anything.

And he didn't say a word.

My teeth ground. This was *such* a bad idea.

But it wasn't like we had many options.

I shifted to shadow briefly, just long enough to get inside the ambulance. When nothing else happened, I extended my hand to Wren. She jumped inside, gripping my palm tightly to keep from falling back against any of the anti-vampire-treated metal. Outside, Liam eyed the wolves as if waiting for one of them to try something.

Axel never stopped grinning. Gunnar simply backed into the corner of the ambulance interior, giving us as much room as his enormous frame could.

Trying not to scowl, I studied the compartment in the floor below us. It'd be cramped. Hell, it'd make us sardines.

"We need to help Ulysses and Gideon," Wren whispered as if picking up on my reluctance.

I nodded.

"How long will this take?" she continued to the wolves.

"Depends." Silas shrugged. "The GSS is patrolling the city—beneath human radar—and rabids are everywhere. The compartment is shielded, but if we want to avoid closer examination by the slayers' toys or your brethren's senses, it would be smart to steer clear of them both as best we can. Thus our path will be... circuitous."

Logical. Also annoying as hell, since it only meant we'd be smashed into this tiny box for longer.

Dammit.

I lowered myself into the compartment, shifting around to make room as Wren came down to join me. She nestled in close, and I wrapped my arms around her, hating how vulnerable this left us in relation to the shifters.

In shadow form, Liam poured into the compartment as well. Once he was in position behind her, he shifted again, scowling the moment he returned to his human shape.

Gunnar said nothing as he closed the panel, but Axel's voice carried past the metal walls. "Vampires in a box." The psychopath cackled.

My arms tightened around Wren. If there'd been *any* other way to get into St. Louis...

I heard a door open, and the ambulance rocked gently when someone climbed inside. A vibration carried through the metal compartment as the engine started, and even if I knew it was irrational, I still wished there was a window in this thing, if only to let us know we weren't being completely betrayed.

The ambulance began moving, and the sound of garage doors clanking came from up ahead. I couldn't smell anything through the tight compartment and all sound from outside was muffled by the metal. It was like being in a coffin, and unlike all of the myths about our kind, we didn't enjoy lying in those.

Too close to actually being dead.

The seconds turned into minutes and crept onward. I focused on using every ounce of training and discipline I had gathered over my nine-hundred-plus years to remain calm so as not to worry Wren through our connection. She was anxious, I could tell. In the pitch black, her hands gripped me, and the anxiety pulsed through the link between us. On her other side, Liam rubbed her arm, clearly trying to soothe her, but his energy was like a caged animal just waiting for the door to open so that he could lunge out again.

After an eternity of random turns, stops, and starts, the ambulance came to a halt. The driver's door opened and then shut while a clunk came from the lock of the compartment panel above us.

Gunnar pulled the metal aside and extended his hand to Wren. At a low, threatening growl from Liam, the large wolf's eyebrow twitched up, but he stepped back, his hand raised in a gesture as if to say he meant no harm.

The back of the ambulance opened as we climbed from the compartment. Silas regarded us calmly while behind him, Axel surveyed what looked like an alleyway.

He still wore that same mad grin. I wondered if he could stop.

I shoved the irrelevant thought aside. "Where are we?" I asked Silas.

"About a mile from downtown," he replied. "Vampires seem to be holding territory south of here, if the movements of the GSS are any indication. If your guys are still in the city, that's probably where you'll find them."

I jumped down from the ambulance, studying our surroundings. The brick walls on either side of us were pasted with disintegrating flyers. Ordinary sounds of a city at night carried through the cool autumn air—a siren in the distance, the laughter of drunks, and the whisper of intermittent late-night traffic. A stray tabby cat crouched beside an overflowing garbage bin, hissing furiously at the wolf shifters.

"Here, kitty," Axel teased, inching closer to it.

Silas ignored him while the tabby ran for its life. "We'll wait for two hours, and then we're heading back."

"Any checkpoints nearby?" I asked.

"At least one that way." He nodded to the west. "But as I said before, they're changing them all the time. No guarantees where they might be now."

I ground my teeth at the response, but there wasn't anything for it. And we were closer to Ulysses and Gideon than we'd been before.

It had to be enough.

"Let's go," I said to Wren and Liam.

Wren paused. "Thank you," she told the wolves.

Silas smiled with polite professionalism. "Don't be late."

Nodding nervously, Wren followed us as we headed for the opening of the alleyway. At the edge, I peered out, checking around swiftly but seeing nothing.

"Can you feel Gideon or Ulysses?" I asked Wren in a low voice, though I knew the shifters would probably overhear us anyway. Their hearing was notorious.

She glanced around, biting her lip anxiously, and then closed her eyes. Seconds crept past, and then suddenly she jerked back, her eyes flying open again.

"That way." She pointed to the right. "I'm not sure where, though. Not far."

"Who is it?" Liam asked in a rough whisper.

Uncertainty tinged her expression. "Ulysses... I think."

Liam and I shared a short look. Even if she could still feel him, that didn't mean anything for whether he was safe. He'd been with Amalie for weeks now. We'd seen him in those videos.

The moment he spotted us, he might try to kill us. And then we'd have only one choice.

If it came down to it, we'd destroy him to protect her, even if it meant it would destroy us too.

27

ULYSSES

The tunnels were gone, and the rocky terrain too. On a scrap of a ledge, I stood, my hands clinging to the rocks. Emptiness surrounded me like a gaping void that had no end. In it, there was just this small scrap of rock and this tiny ledge of a cliff.

One fragment of me, left at the end of my universe.

Screams echoed through the nothingness—the endless howls of the dying. Hot moisture splattered me—their blood hitting my face, right before I bit them and swallowed the rest down. Like an aurora borealis made out of a horror movie, the images played across the face of the endless abyss. Over and over, I saw the way so many cried and screamed and begged to be spared.

And how I never did.

I'd never wanted to be a killer. I knew that much about my life, even if everything else was gone. I'd cared about people. Wanted to help them because they mattered to me.

Now I just wished I could remember anyone at all.

An odd sensation suddenly threaded through the darkness, and my attention snapped up. I knew this. The sound was like the murmur of a familiar friend, finally returned to me. And it was precious. I'd longed for it before I even knew what it was. I'd searched for her for lifetimes.

I went still inside myself. *Her.*

Different images flared to life in the void, colorless and blurred like a recording from long ago. A cliff. A woman. The sun burning down on us, scorching her to ash. But she wasn't gone, not anymore. She'd come back to us twice, once so horribly wrong and once so perfectly right.

Wren.

Joy like the sun rising through clouds surged inside me at her name. Oh, gods, I remembered her. And with her, others too. Men who were like brothers to me, who I'd fight for and die for a thousand times over out of love for them. We'd been bound together across lifetimes, united and equal and...

Sentinels.

The word reverberated, as if every cell of my being knew we were called by that name. All around me, more of the cliff emerged from the nothingness, the edge of the mountain upon which I stood slowly returning from the abyss.

"What are you doing?" a voice echoed through the darkness.

Rage roared hot in an instant at the sound. Amalie. She'd gone so wrong, this scrap of our history. This twisted queen who'd found us and chained us to her, preferring slaves to lovers and torture to anything resembling kindness.

But if she was asking that…

Oh, gods. Was this affecting my body too?

Gripping the cliff face, I grunted and strained to drag myself up and away from the abyss, though I didn't know where there was to go. But I had to regain control of my muscles. Wren was out there.

Fading.

Desperation crushed in on me. My sense of her was disappearing, pulling away so fast, I couldn't hope to catch up to it.

I wanted to howl.

Hands snagged my face, digging into my skin. Amalie's scowl came into view in the void. I couldn't move my body, but I also knew my body wasn't trying to lash out and hurt anyone. I'd gone as still as a mannequin, immobile, which was better than killing people.

Her eyes stared into mine. "She's there, isn't she? That little bitch is back again." Amalie's lips curled into a snarl. "Where is she?"

She searched my face. I prayed I was giving nothing away, not that I knew what there was to reveal.

"Close?" Her eyes narrowed, and her suspicious expression turned to a grin. "Okay. Let's see how she likes those fangs of yours now, eh?"

Amalie released me sharply, and dread rolled through me. I wanted to stop her, but she was already striding away from me and my body was following her like a nightmarish puppet.

But she was going to hurt Wren.

Or I was.

With a snarl, I dragged myself higher on the cliff face. I couldn't let the void win. I had to regain control of my body, even if only for long enough to wrap myself in lead weights and throw myself into the ocean.

I had to protect Wren.

Even if it was from myself.

28

GIDEON

I'd hung so long from these chains that I was fairly certain I was going to lose use of my hands entirely. Friday and Barnaby were still alive, though, if only barely. Amalie seemed to have abandoned the idea of killing them. Abandoned everything, really. Neither she nor Urlfeige had dragged me into their presence or showed their face since Amalie raced out of here some unknown amount of time ago.

But the rabids made up for it. They'd turned torturing the demons for fun into a veritable sport, just to see me try to save them. At least the pair of bastards in here now had grown bored fairly early, stopping the torment and now leaning against the wall as if wondering what they'd done to deserve such dull guard duty. I didn't recognize them, but from the ragged nature of their clothes and overall appearance, I suspected they had started this way, rather than being turned into monsters like so many others.

Not that it mattered that they ignored me. The chains were bolted to the wall by more than steel and stone. Magic held them there, and all of my straining hadn't succeeded in breaking them.

Warmth carried through my mind, like the whisper I'd heard before, but stronger. More... real somehow.

My head snapped up. It was Wren. I knew it without question. She was here—and close.

Horror spread through me like a cold wave. Oh, gods, had the rabids captured her?

My arms were straining at the chains before I even finished registering the thought. By all that was holy, if Amalie had caught her, if Ulysses had hurt her... or, gods, Urlfeige...

I snarled, hauling on the stone and metal as shouts came from beyond the door. Amalie's voice rang out, shouting orders, sounding furious.

Hope flared inside me. That wasn't her tone for when things were going well, which meant maybe Wren was free. Were Asher and Liam with her?

The thought bore its own horror. If they weren't and something had happened to them, and I hadn't been there to stop it...

I twisted my wrists to wrap my hands around the chains, willing life back into my numb fingers. The magic-bound metal burned my palms, and I hissed through my teeth at the pain.

At least my nerves still worked.

"Hey!" The rabid's voice carried across the room. "What the hell are you doing?"

I ignored him, tightening my grip as best I could.

"I'm talking to you, traitor." The rabid pushed to his feet, and his companion did the same. "You want us to fry these bats?"

In her cell of magic bars, Friday's eyes locked on me, but I didn't see fear in her gaze. More like readiness. She knew something had changed. So long sharing a house meant we could read each other well.

"Dammit, traitor." The rabid hit the button on the key fob. Friday screamed as the bars around her flared to life. "You like that?"

He released the button, and Friday sagged back to the floor.

"Whatever it is," the demon gasped breathlessly. "Do what you need to do."

The rabid looked between us. "No talking!" He hit the button again, and her screams rang from the walls.

Rage flooded through me. I couldn't let them kill the demons, and I couldn't let Amalie catch Wren.

No, I needed to *find* Wren, if only to try to understand why she meant so much to me.

Because she wasn't Amalie. She never had been. And for too long, I'd let my fear of the queen rob me of the chance to be with her.

Just as we'd once been.

That last thought was irrational, but I didn't care. I'd been trapped by Amalie in heart and spirit more than I ever realized, even after my body had escaped her.

I wouldn't let myself be trapped again.

I gripped the chains and strained against the wall. The rabids hit their little buttons, and Friday and Barnaby both screamed. Adrenaline flooded my arms and muscles as I pulled harder.

Old words fell from my lips. I didn't recognize the language, only the impulse to speak them.

Stone cracked. The chains tore from their moorings, sending me tumbling forward. The rabids shouted, abandoning the key fobs as they charged forward to stop me.

I lunged at them, and my tired hands grabbed the nearest one, ripping out his throat. The other stumbled back, but I wasn't done. Charging forward, I grasped him by the neck, quickly doing the same.

Blood covered my fingers and dripped from my chest where the arterial spray had caught me, but there were more important matters right now than whether I looked like a horror show. Turning, I strode over to the metal cells and gripped the bars. The magic scorched my palms, burning, and I snarled at the pain. Yanking hard, I muttered the words again, and then roared with triumph as I ripped one of the bars free. Friday slipped past quickly, eyeing me with a strange look before heading for her husband.

I had no breath left in me, and my heart had long since gone still. Exhaustion bore down on me like lead weights. I growled, fighting it as I crossed the distance to Barnaby's cage.

The bar clattered away at my sharp yank. Friday slipped through the gap swiftly to help her husband to his feet. Together, the demons hobbled out of the cell again.

"Wren is out there," I grunted past the throbbing of my palms.

"Where did you learn that language?" she asked.

I shook my head. "I don't know."

After a heartbeat, Friday nodded. "Let's find your Wren."

I glanced between them. She could barely stand, and Barnaby was much the same. I couldn't bring them to a fight. Not when they could get captured again. "You should just get out of here."

"What?" Friday stared at me. "We can help, dear. Just give us a minute and—"

"I won't risk you."

Her eyes slid to her husband, worry in her gaze.

"We can help," Barnaby repeated his wife's words firmly.

I grimaced. "Keep watch from a distance," I said. "Help me if you can, but stay out of the line of fire. Please."

Friday shared a look with her husband and then nodded. Staggering toward me, she put a hand to my cheek. "You are a good man, Gideon."

My lips twitched, but I knew it wasn't true. Not really. I'd made so many mistakes. But as I headed for the door with both of them behind me, I swore to myself that at least with Wren, I wouldn't make any more.

29

<hr>

WREN

Half the time, I felt like a kid playing a make-believe game of "monsters are hunting me." Sneaking through the city streets like enemies would burst from the walls was surreal, especially because everything around me seemed so ordinary. Shops were closed for the night, business offices too, and the smell of late-night pizza and beer hung on the air, making the adrenaline pounding through me seem like a byproduct of my own silly imagination.

But then Asher or Liam would suddenly yank me out of sight because vampires or slayers or God knew who else were up ahead.

And nothing about this felt like a game at all.

Plastered to the side of a building of gray granite and marble, I shivered as Liam peered around a corner, watching the utterly ordinary party girls we'd spotted leaving a bar up ahead. A few blocks back, it'd been a couple of homeless men who'd sent us into hiding for the fifteen minutes it took them to amble on down the street.

"Bounty hunters," Asher had whispered to me when we saw them. And despite the laughter and teasing carrying down the street, making the group of girls sound for all the world like a bunch of drunk sorority sisters, they apparently were bounty hunters too.

I pressed my hands to the cool granite. I couldn't feel Ulysses or Gideon any better now, and nothing around me seemed to indicate vampires were anywhere nearby. But we were closing in on the part of town Silas had said was "vampire territory," and surely that had to count for something.

His eyes on the street beyond the turn, Liam motioned for us to start moving again.

"Are we getting close?" Asher whispered to me as we followed him.

I took a deep breath, trying to feel for Gideon or Ulysses. It was hard to concentrate when I felt like at any moment the GSS or bounty hunters for this Consortium thing could find us, though.

I shook my head. "I'm not sure. I can't really—"

Rabids dropped from the sky.

My sword was in my hand instantly. Plummeting toward the earth in black smoke and shadow, the creatures turned to human form at the last moment. Fangs bared, they grinned at us from all sides.

Their knives gripped in their fists, Asher and Liam spun to take up positions on either side of me. I adjusted my hold on the sword, the blade radiating a white glow like moonlight.

But my hand shook at the sight of Doctor Sissoko among the rabids. She'd helped me when I first woke as a vampire. She'd been there for my family after I escaped Amalie. A few of the nurses I recognized from her clinic were in the crowd as well.

To a person, they looked ready to rip my throat out.

"Steady, Wren," Asher murmured.

I didn't know how to respond. If they attacked... if we had to kill them...

A dark chuckle carried from beyond the rabids ahead of me. Without taking their eyes from us, the crowd parted.

Amalie walked through the opening, Ulysses at her side.

Cold dread sank into me, making me want to cry. That wasn't Ulysses, not really. His eyes were cold. Dead. They stared through us like we were less than nothing. Every trace of his humor and his cocksure smile were gone, replaced by a wooden emptiness that made him look like a mannequin come to life.

"My pet told me you were coming." Amalie stroked her fingertips over his cheek. "He tells me so many things."

Fury surged up to overwhelm my horror like a red-hot wave.

Like hell she'd pretend to *own* him.

Amalie's gaze slid to Asher and Liam. "I'll deal with you naughty boys soon. But first"—she glanced at Ulysses and then turned a grin on me—"kill the girl."

He surged forward like an unleashed attack dog, with no hesitation or sign he recognized me at all. Asher and

Liam moved to intercept him, but the rabids leapt at them immediately. In shadow and human form alike, they swarmed around the two Sentinels, trying to overwhelm them.

I retreated fast. "Please," I cried, torn between lifting my sword to defend myself and the fact it was *Ulysses* I'd be striking. "Fight this. Don't—"

He slammed into me, driving me back to the ground. His weight trapped me against the concrete, his fangs glinted in the streetlights. I struggled to throw him off, my body frantically summoning all the skills I'd learned with Asher and anything Tau knew besides. But Ulysses had been training for centuries, longer than me or an ancient princess. Swiftly, he pinned me, one hand gripping my wrist and twisting sharply.

I shrieked as pain shot through my arm and fingers, and my hold on my sword loosened. With lightning speed, he grabbed for the weapon.

Our hands collided on the hilt.

His eyes went wide. A bolt of pure energy shot through me, as if all the world suddenly blazed with light. In an instant, the bond between us roared to life, stealing everything I could see.

But I could still feel.

Light poured from me into Ulysses, like everything in me had become pure energy. The power surged through him, twisting this way and that, as if he held an eternity of emptiness inside. But the energy within me didn't care about that. Like a heat-seeking missile, it sped deeper into him, searching for something it *knew* was there.

And found it.

Far down within his own mind, a speck of the man I knew still clung to life amid the dark, like a star hanging on against the night. But he wasn't alone. The emptiness wasn't emptiness at all, but a wall of pure nothing, and on its other side lay his blade. Black threads bound it like vines of poison and acid, keeping the emptiness between him and the blade and stopping the knife from returning to him as it wanted.

The threads radiated with Urlfeige's energy. His power. His control.

Oh, hell, no.

Fury poured from me like white-hot fire. The black threads spasmed and tightened, fighting to keep their hold.

My hand clenched down on my sword. The sounds of battle around me faded away. The concrete and the night as well. There was only me and Ulysses and a damned old man who still thought he could control us millennia after he should have died.

A deep and angry snarl carried through my mind. That bastard was fighting me. But still, the threads grew brittle, grew thin.

And snapped.

A blast wave of white light rushed out at me. Suddenly, I was carried backward, out from Ulysses and into my own body.

I blinked hard, my vision swirling but gradually becoming clear. I was on my back on the rough concrete. The sound of my own heart was loud in my ears, muffling the noise of shrieking all around.

Ulysses was staring down at me.

A breath rushed from my chest. It was him, there in his own eyes. Not that dead thing. Not that feral and murderous attack dog.

"Wren?" he whispered.

I choked on a sob. "It's you."

He nodded, his expression lost somewhere between wonder and pain. "You—"

A shrieking shadow swept past us, colliding with a wall. Awareness of our situation seemed to hit him suddenly, and he shot to his feet. His knife appeared in his hand, the blade glowing like pure white fire against the darkness. On shaky legs, I scrambled up after him, my sword rematerializing in my fist.

Asher and Liam were still fighting to reach us. I couldn't tell among the shadow forms of rabids whether the doctor or anyone we knew was still alive.

From the other side of the battle, Amalie stared at us.

I'd swear there was fear in her eyes.

Her face twitched. "Wh... wha..."

Ulysses put himself between me and her, his knife at the ready.

She gave a ragged shriek, her lips pulling back in a snarl. "You little *bitch*!"

Black smoke surged from the ground around her, pouring up like she'd opened the pits of hell.

As one, the rabids paused, several of them shifting back to human form like even they were shocked by what she'd done. I spotted the doctor. Several nurses too. They still looked crazed, and when the smoke rolled toward them, they didn't move, like they were suddenly at a loss for what they were supposed to be doing.

The smoke brushed across the nearest of the rabids.

Skin and bone turned to ash. They barely even managed to scream before they died.

Shrieking with terror, Doctor Sissoko and the rest of the rabids took to the sky, fleeing fast.

Amalie never even spared them a glance, her eyes still locked on me. "You think you've *won* something?"

Firelight flared in the smoke around her. Strange shapes twisted in the churning darkness, and as one, Asher and Liam retreated toward us, staying clear of it all.

At the motion, incredulous rage and more than a little confusion flashed over Amalie's face. "You're *mine*," she spat at them. "My possessions. My Sentinels."

Her eyes snapped back to me, and fear flashed in their depths again. She didn't know how I'd freed Ulysses, I realized.

Or maybe where I'd found the strength.

"You think you've taken anything?" she snarled. "That they're yours now? You're *nothing*. Precious little *Tau* is nothing. I kept that pathetic princess bound in my mind for centuries while I learned more magic than she could ever dream existed. And her father? *My* father?" Something dark and strange swept across her eyes. "He taught me more still."

She flung her hand out toward me. A bolt of black energy flew from her palm, twisting through the air like a snake.

Asher and Liam lunged to intercept it while Ulysses spun, shoving me aside.

It wasn't enough.

The power whipped between them to slam into my

chest, throwing me backward. Pain screamed through my body, burning across my vision in a wave of white and red light. I couldn't breathe. Couldn't think. I crashed into something hard, my head cracking against it.

And then there was only darkness.

30

ULYSSES

The black bolt of magic collided with Wren, hurling her back. I dove after her immediately, but my body couldn't shift, couldn't move fast enough. She slammed into the bricks and crumpled to the ground like a ragdoll.

One with a spear of pure darkness sticking up from her chest, right above her heart.

I crashed to my knees at her side, while a roar of pure rage came from behind me. Asher's fury flooded through the connection between us, overwhelming after so long trapped in the cold, solitary hell of my own mind.

But I was back. Free.

And Wren was dying.

My hands hovered over the spear. Yanking the weapon from her chest could make her bleed out. But leaving it there—

"Get back!" Asher shouted.

I threw a look over my shoulder in time to see the smoke surrounding Amalie surge upward and outward, swallowing her and colliding with the buildings on either side like battering rams. Concrete and steel crumpled inward. The remaining stone and steel teetered for a moment, the wall beneath them gone, before the structures began to crumble.

Oh, shit.

Asher turned to shadow while instantly, Liam did the same.

I didn't have time to question how they'd done it. Scooping Wren up, spear and all, I took off running. That inexplicable sword of hers was gone, vanished into the ether the moment she hit the wall. But she lolled in my grip like everything in her was broken, and I couldn't stand it.

She'd make it, though. I wouldn't get back to her only to lose her an instant later.

And she wouldn't die all because she'd tried to save me.

Her body suddenly spasmed in my arms like she was being shocked. As if they were boneless, her limbs twitched and jerked. I glanced down and nearly stumbled in horror to see a black stain spreading around the spear, like ink seeping straight into her skin.

"Hang on, baby," I begged her, wishing I could slow down long enough to yank the weapon from her—or that I'd already done that when I had the fucking chance. "Hang on."

I darted around a corner as a wave of dust and grit

thundered past behind me. Clutching her tightly, I kept running past office buildings and restaurants closed for the night until finally the ground stopped shaking and the roar of falling steel and concrete faded from the world.

Breathing hard, I threw a look back as my feet slowed. I couldn't see any sign of Amalie. Rabids either.

"Put her down, put her down."

I turned to see Asher in human form ahead of me, motioning fast for me to lower Wren to the sidewalk. Nearby, Liam shifted back as well, his entire body quivering like he needed to attack something, *anything* if only it would help.

Quickly, I laid Wren down, trying to be gentle. But the spasms were getting worse, and her skin was like ice. "Hold her. I'll grab the—"

"Oh, gods."

My attention snapped over at the sound of Gideon's voice. Dust clouds swirling around him, he stood on the street ahead of us, his horrified gaze locked on Wren. Friday and Barnaby were behind him, helping each other stand, but at the sight of us, Barnaby nudged his wife forward. Friday hurried across the road, obviously unsteady on her feet.

"Don't you dare touch that," she chided, lowering herself down on the other side of Wren. "I haven't seen something like this in millennia, and I doubt it's become friendlier since then."

"We have to get it out of her," I insisted.

"Now, did I say to leave the girl like that?" She glared at me. Her skin had a grayish tinge and her face was gaunt. A red sheen touched her eyes like her hold on her human form was slipping. "Get back."

I scrambled backward immediately.

Gritting her teeth, Friday braced herself and then grasped the spear. A snarl left her that reached right down into some primordial part of my brain and made it demand I run for my life.

But like hell I'd listen to that when Wren's life was at stake.

With a sharp jerk, Friday yanked the spear free and tossed it aside. "Stay away from that," she snapped.

"What the hell was it doing to her?" Asher demanded.

Friday made an uncertain noise.

I didn't take my eyes from Wren. She wasn't turning to dust, which meant she wasn't dead. And the spasms were fading, her body easing back onto the concrete like the burgeoning seizure finally had stopped.

But that black stain on her chest wasn't fading, and she sure as hell wasn't waking up.

"Any sign of Amalie?" Barnaby asked us.

Asher shook his head, but I didn't miss how his eyes flicked over to me, weighing.

I didn't blame him. I wouldn't trust me either.

Memories tugged at the edge of my concentration, as if my mind wanted to recap hell now that it could think clearly again, offering additional proof that Asher's doubt was right.

Like I needed that.

Like Wren fucking did.

"So now what?" I said, my voice tight as I shoved the flashes of blood and horror aside. "How do we help her?"

"We have a way out of town," Asher admitted after a moment. "If we can make it to the—"

Shrieks and growls echoed down the street in either direction, cutting him off.

Chills ran through me. My memories were still spotty, but that sounded like more rabids than had been on the street with Amalie a few minutes ago.

A *lot* more.

"Might I suggest we continue this elsewhere?" Barnaby said, tension breaking past his carefully measured tone.

Gideon jerked his head at the street behind him. "I spotted somewhere defensible not far from here."

Asher eyed him a moment before his gaze flicked to Friday and Barnaby, and I'd known the man long enough to read his utter lack of expression.

He wasn't one hundred percent sure he could trust Gideon either.

Ignoring all of us, Liam moved fast, scooping Wren from the ground and cradling her close.

I blinked, alarmed. He was good with that now? The touching thing?

What else had changed while I was some nightmare puppet for Amalie?

I shoved the thought aside. There'd be time for that later. Now, the shrieks were coming closer, and whatever else Asher thought of us, that sound seemed to decide it for him.

His knife blazed to life in his fist. "Let's get the hell out of here."

Thank you for reading Blood Rebel! Wren and the Sentinels' story concludes in Blood Queen: Book Four of the Vampire Rebellion Series.

ABOUT THE AUTHOR

Sierra Rowan is the author of action-packed reverse harem paranormal romance and urban fantasy novels. They love to write stories filled with steam, heart, and adventure where a happily-ever-after is guaranteed, even if it takes some magical battles and car chases to get there.

Get updates about all of Sierra's books at sierrarowan.com.

amazon.com/author/sierrarowan

bookbub.com/authors/sierra-rowan

goodreads.com/sierrarowan

facebook.com/authorsierrarowan

instagram.com/authorsierrarowan

tiktok.com/@sierrarowanbooks

twitter.com/SierraRowanBook